Bolan catfoot
heading for the skylight

He unclipped three smoke grenades and set them on the metal roof, within arm's reach. That done, he opened the canvas satchel, set the timer and closed the flap again. The basic charge was C-4 plastique, with a hot incendiary kicker to ensure maximum destruction when it blew.

With the Beretta set for 3-round burst, he pulled the trigger twice, watched the plate-glass box disintegrate, dropped the satchel and got out of there.

The warrior scrambled down the ladder, already halfway to the bottom when he heard the sound of running feet below. He hung on with one hand, drew the heavy Magnum with the other and swiveled to meet the threat.

Two Nomads were below him, both with weapons up and ready. The Desert Eagle bellowed twice, 240 grains of death taking both gunners out of play.

The C-4 blast was slightly muffled by the building, but it raised the roof. The metal walls bowed, rippling visibly. The thermite charge flung white-hot coals around the interior, burning everything they touched. If there was any screaming from the center of the funeral pyre, Bolan didn't hear it.

The heat was on, and the Executioner was turning up the fire.

MACK BOLAN®

The Executioner

DON PENDLETON'S THE EXECUTIONER®

FEATURING MACK BOLAN

COLORS OF HELL

A GOLD EAGLE BOOK FROM
WORLDWIDE®

TORONTO • NEW YORK • LONDON
AMSTERDAM • PARIS • SYDNEY • HAMBURG
STOCKHOLM • ATHENS • TOKYO • MILAN
MADRID • WARSAW • BUDAPEST • AUCKLAND

First edition June 1992

ISBN 0-373-61162-5

Special thanks and acknowledgment to
Mike Newton for his contribution to this work.

COLORS OF HELL

Crime leaves a trail like a water beetle:
Like a snail, it leaves its shine:
Like a horse mango, it leaves its reek.

—Malay proverb

Fear succeeds crime—it is its punishment.

—Voltaire

I've followed the trail of crime back to its source,
and the time for punishment has arrived. It's time
for the savages to live in fear for a change.

—Mack Bolan

THE
MACK BOLAN®
LEGEND

Nothing less than a war could have fashioned the destiny of the man called Mack Bolan. Bolan earned the Executioner title in the jungle hell of Vietnam.

But this soldier also wore another name—Sergeant Mercy. He was so tagged because of the compassion he showed to wounded comrades-in-arms and Vietnamese civilians.

Mack Bolan's second tour of duty ended prematurely when he was given emergency leave to return home and bury his family, victims of the Mob. Then he declared a one-man war against the Mafia.

He confronted the Families head-on from coast to coast, and soon a hope of victory began to appear. But Bolan had broken society's every rule. That same society started gunning for this elusive warrior—to no avail.

So Bolan was offered amnesty to work within the system against terrorism. This time, as an employee of Uncle Sam, Bolan became Colonel John Phoenix. With a command center at Stony Man Farm in Virginia, he and his new allies—Able Team and Phoenix Force—waged relentless war on a new adversary: the KGB.

But when his one true love, April Rose, died at the hands of the Soviet terror machine, Bolan severed all ties with Establishment authority.

Now, after a lengthy lone-wolf struggle and much soul-searching, the Executioner has agreed to enter an "arm's-length" alliance with his government once more, reserving the right to pursue personal missions in his Everlasting War.

1

It was one mile from Hunters Point to Candlestick Park as the crow flies across South Basin. Driving, it was roughly twice as far. But there were children on the Point who grew to middle age without a firsthand visit to the stadium, much less a look inside. The Point was San Francisco's ghetto, and for many, if not most, of its inhabitants the neighborhood was both their prison and their world. A bloody riot in the sixties had wrought no major change in Hunters Point, where unemployment, poverty and crime were still the basic facts of life.

Mack Bolan knew the story, or as much of it as any white man would ever really know. He understood that poverty was both a motivating factor and, at times, a lame excuse for rampant crime. Some men would steal to feed their families, as others turned to drink or drugs for some relief from the perpetual humiliation of the unemployed. Some unwed mothers sold themselves to make the rent or feed the kids.

The flip side was a seamy world of crack cocaine and gangs who preyed on the community at large, without a trace of social conscience. Pimps and pushers, thieves and teenage killers, they'd spend their dirty money on stereos, gold jewelry or a brand-new Cadillac before they helped a homeless family pay the rent. When they were busted with a load of coke or automatic weapons, they employed slick lawyers and immediately raised the cry of prejudice and police harassment. In fact, they cared no more about their race than if they'd been bred in test tubes.

A predator was still a predator, in any color of the rainbow. As it happened, these were black.

The meet at Candlestick had been his contact's notion, and the Executioner approached it warily. The guy was squeaky clean, according to police and Bolan's source at Justice, but survival on the edge meant double-checking every stranger, testing each new step for snares or booby traps. How many times had the warrior seen a local "Mr. Clean" with dirt beneath his fingernails?

Too many, right.

He drove the rental car south on Giants Drive and picked up Jamestown Avenue, then north on Hunters Point Expressway to complete the loop. The route let Bolan check the parking lot around the stadium for plants. A couple of dozen cars were parked together on the north side—maintenance employees working on the grounds—and one sedan that stuck out like a sore thumb on the south.

A Plymouth Fury, navy blue.

His contact.

Bolan pulled into the parking lot and stopped two hundred yards away. Field glasses brought the Fury kissing close, and the warrior concentrated on the man behind the wheel. The grainy photocopy of his driver's license photo didn't do him justice, but the faces were the same.

There was no way of telling whether someone was hunched down behind the driver's seat, or huddled in the trunk. It was a gamble Bolan had to take if he intended to pursue the matter any farther than he had.

He recognized a touch of paranoia, after what went down in Baton Rouge, but that was natural. The game had nearly blown up in his face, the closest thing he'd ever seen to a quadruple cross, and the disturbing memories were barely two days old. He had no reason to believe that any of the players left alive were still at liberty, but some things weren't easily forgotten.

It had begun with drugs in Baton Rouge, and the suspicion of a local sheriff's captain watching over shipments from Colombia. Investigation proved that the suspicions were correct, but there was more to Baton Rouge than met the eye. Not only was the sheriff's captain dirty, but his operation was infringing on the territory of a mafioso who'd gone into partnership with members of the state police, a congressman and others to eliminate the competition with a minimum of personal exposure. They were setting up Justice to do the job, and Justice had, in turn, requested Hal Brognola's team from Stony Man to see what might be done about the situation, as a favor to the local team.

It had been close for a while, with Bolan's hands tied by his solemn pledge that he'd never drop the hammer on a cop, no matter how that officer disgraced his shield. Brognola's team was mopping up, and the big Fed predicted sweeping prosecutions at the federal level, but the Executioner had learned that victories were fleeting in his private war.

You plugged one leak and turned around to find three others pumping sewage in its place. The savages you killed or caged today were instantly replaced by others waiting in the wings.

Some days he felt like giving up, a natural reaction in the circumstances, but he never let the feeling put down roots. If there were any doubts in Bolan's mind about the value of his war, he had only to think about the victims, crying out for help and justice, to renew his own determination for the right.

Like now.

He tucked the glasses underneath his seat and picked up his Ingram submachine gun. It was a compact weapon, about eleven inches overall without the MAC silencer attached, and its prodigious cyclic rate of fire would empty out a 32-round magazine in almost a second and a half. It took an expert hand to use the Ingram for precision work, but there was nothing like it for a bit of close-up action in emergencies.

He lifted off the rental's brake and started creeping toward the Fury, one hand on the steering wheel, the other on the Ingram in his lap. If it came down to killing, he could hose the Plymouth and be out of there in four, five seconds flat.

He pulled up on the driver's side, the Fury's window cranking down as he approached. His contact was a black man, thirty-nine years old according to his operator's license, with a trace of gray in his hair around the temples.

"Good morning, Mr. Souders."

"Mr. Blanski, I presume?" His voice was deep enough to hold the bass line in a choir.

"The very same."

"If I could have a look at your credentials, please...."

"I'm here. Your first name's Vernon, and I know your face."

"Too many people know my face and name these days."

"Okay."

The laminated card identified one Michael Blanski as a member of a nonexistent federal agency attached to Justice. Callback numbers out of Stony Man Farm would prop up the cover, but any search in depth would meet dead ends and break the phony Justice link without embarrassment to anyone of consequence in Washington. There was no photograph of Bolan on the card.

The card changed hands and came back a moment later with the makings of a weary smile. "Your place or mine?"

"I'll drive. You talk."

"Sounds fair."

Bolan kept the Ingram in his lap while Souders locked the Plymouth, circling around the rental to the passenger side, but it was safely out of sight before his passenger got in, a well-worn briefcase in hand.

"I really didn't think anyone would come."

"You asked for help," Bolan said, releasing the brake. "I'm here."

"One man."

"How many do you need?"

"Right now an army wouldn't hurt."

Before he could respond the Executioner picked up a bogey, in his rearview mirror. The chase car was a Datsun pickup, jacked so low that it barely cleared the ground.

"You bring an escort?" Bolan asked.

"No way." His passenger glanced around, blinking once. "Well, shit."

The warrior stood on the accelerator, leaving rubber on the pavement as he held a narrow lead. The Datsun hung in right behind him, and while he couldn't see the driver because of tinted windows, Bolan spotted two dark figures rising from the open truck bed, weapons in hand.

"Get down!"

The rental took a few hits on the trunk as Bolan started weaving, throwing off his adversaries' aim.

The nearest exit from the parking lot put Bolan on the Jamestown Avenue extension, with a choice of turning left or right. He thought about the morning traffic back in town and took the left, heading for another loop around the stadium with room to make his play before he brought the shooters into contact with civilians.

In the shotgun seat his passenger was hunched down like a pro in order to minimize his silhouette. It looked as if Vernon Souders had been under fire before.

They reached the exit, and Bolan took a moment to retrieve the Ingram. Souders blinked again, was seemingly about to speak, then reconsidered.

"Who are they?" Bolan snapped.

"I didn't get a look. It could be Skulls or Nomads, either way."

The names were familiar, recalled from Brognola's thumbnail briefing on the phone, the warrior realized it made no difference which gang had dispatched the firing squad. Both took pride in the efficiency with which they killed their enemies, and if a few bystanders fell along the way, well, what the hell?

He also knew that some of them were teenagers, a few no more than children.

At the moment Bolan didn't dwell on it.

In front of him and closing fast was a sharp left to the Hunters Point Expressway. It had been only moments since he'd driven this route the first time, scouting out the territory for his meet with Souders, and the layout was imprinted on his mind. Three hundred yards downrange, on Bolan's right, was the entrance to a parking lot for Bay View Park.

"Hang on!"

Bolan took the hard right doing fifty, two wheels lifting off the pavement for a heartbeat, then settling again with force enough to snap his teeth together. Up ahead and on his left stood an unoccupied Parks Department truck. The only vehicle in Bolan's way.

He hit the brakes and cranked the steering wheel to put the rental through a right bootlegger's turn, one-eighty with the rubber smoking. They would up facing back in the direction of the street, in time to see the Datsun pickup rolling in.

The warrior had his window down and the Ingram in his left hand as he stood on the accelerator, giving his assailants no time to consider what their options ought to be. Beside him Vernon Souders braced himself against the dashboard with a stiff right arm, lips moving silently in prayer.

The driver of the Datsun saw him coming, and he wasn't backing down from anybody. Burning off the mark, the pickup held a steady course to pass a yard or so on Bolan's left. The gunners in the back could score at that range, even if they didn't aim.

At thirty yards and closing the Executioner let the Ingram rip, a short burst punching through the smoky windshield, driver's side, and tracking on to let the shooters have the rest of it. Without its silencer the little submachine gun sounded like a power saw, and the effect of high-speed Parabellum slugs at close to point-blank range was pretty much the same.

The Datsun's windshield blew, mangled hollow-points and fractured glass exploding in the driver's face. He lost it, reaching up to save his eyes. The deceleration of the pickup threw his shooters in the back off balance, ruining their aims.

The second burst from Bolan's stuttergun came in around chest-high and caught them both with dazed expressions on their faces. They were dead before they knew it, with the impact of the Parabellum manglers slamming both hardguys over onto their backs and out of sight.

Bolan started to brake instantly, yawing into another smoking turn and rocking to a halt a few yards from the entrance to the parking lot. The Datsun kept on going, clocking maybe six or seven miles per hour with a dead man at the wheel, as the warrior fed another magazine into the Ingram.

"What's going on?" Souders asked.

"Sit tight," Bolan said. "We're not done yet."

"Oh, Jesus."

Coming up behind the Datsun, Bolan had his gun arm out the window, ready. He was fairly certain that the riflemen in back were dead, the driver likewise dead or dying, but he took no chances on a rude surprise. When street gang members started packing military hardware, it was possible that some of them wore body armor.

He watched the Datsun ram the Parks Department's truck and heard the engine stall. Still creeping forward, he was ready when the right-hand door flew open and a lanky figure hit the blacktop running, winging two quick shots at Bolan with a .45 automatic.

The warrior swung the rental's steering wheel and nudged the pedal, keeping pace. In front of him the runner veered hard left in the direction of the tree line, pouring on some speed. The Executioner was mulling over whether he should let the young man go, and then his target blew it, swiveling around to try another shot.

Too bad.

The Ingram caught him with a rising burst and set him spinning like a top. He hit the ground and shivered once before the life fled out of him.

All the hitters were taken out.

"I guess we'd better have that talk," Bolan said.

"Jesus Christ."

"Not here."

"I know a place. Oh, God."

2

The first stop, after fetching Souders's Plymouth, was another car rental agency. Souders waited down the block while Bolan hired a brand-new car. They left the first vehicle, cored with bullet holes, at Youngblood Coleman Playground, keys in the ignition.

The Executioner followed Souders to a small apartment house on Bryant Street near Franklin Square. There had been no sign of a tail along the way, but the warrior tucked the Ingram underneath his coat before they went inside.

The place was clean and furnished in a homey style. There were photos on the wall, which might have been family, or simply friends. A message light was winking on the telephone answering machine by the couch, but Souders made no move to check it out.

"My cousin's place," he said in explanation. "He's a salesman and out of town a lot. He has me check things out from time to time, bring in the mail, make sure nobody's messing with his things."

"Okay."

"You want a drink or something? I could use one, after...what just happened."

"No."

He picked a chair and settled in, watching as Souders shed his jacket and moved toward the kitchen. He took a bottle from a cupboard by the fridge and poured himself a double shot. It seemed to help, and the man didn't require another for the short walk to the couch.

"It's not my way to pry, but if you wouldn't mind my asking . . . Do you do this kind of thing a lot?"

"What kind of thing is that?" Bolan asked.

"Have gunfights out by Candlestick."

"I haven't been to San Francisco for a while," the Executioner replied.

"I see."

"You asked for help. I think I understand your problem, but it wouldn't hurt to start from the beginning."

"Right. Okay." Souders spent a silent moment sorting his thoughts, then asked, "I don't suppose you've heard about the Skulls and Nomads?"

"Street gangs? Not specifically. I know they're on the increase up and down the state."

"To put it mildly. Let me take you back a little to the 'good old days.' Let's say two years ago."

There was a bitterness in Souders's tone, a sense of loss that Bolan recognized from other victims, other battle zones.

"That's when the gangs were organized?"

"Oh, we've had gangs forever," Souders replied. "Young punks hanging out and fighting over turf, some vandalism now and then. They smoke some weed or drink some Thunderbird and steal a car, that kind of thing. I'm not about to tell you that they were angels, Mr. Blanski. We've had rapes, some knifings. Now and then somebody wound up dead. But it was nothing like the shit we're living with today."

"I'm listening."

"Around two years ago, the way I hear it from cops downtown, the L.A. gangs were starting to expand. Made so much money selling crack they couldn't spend it all, but still they're wanting more. It's like some kind of poison, how it spreads. They're in Chicago now, I'm told, and Kansas City—everywhere. All coming from Los Angeles."

"Go on."

"The Skulls came first. I couldn't pin down the date for you, any closer than a month, but you could see the difference in graffiti right away. Nobody noticed them recruiting locals, for a while, but then the gangs began to change. You follow me?"

"I do."

"Instead of smoking weed and ripping off a grocery store from time to time, the homeboys started selling crack and packing heat. The beat cops used to confiscate a pistol now and then, but overnight we're talking military weapons, drive-by shootings, crazy stuff like that. Instead of two or three kids murdered every year, we're getting three or four a week."

"You named another gang."

"The Savage Nomads, right. They started moving in a couple of months behind the Skulls. Down south the two gangs fight like cats and dogs. You might have read about it in the papers a year or so ago when half a dozen of the leaders sat down in the L.A. civic auditorium to try to sign a treaty. The reporters and the mayor were kissing up to them like it was General Patton and the Russians shaking hands."

"I understand it didn't take."

"Not even close. These days our children have to watch the clothes they wear to school. The Skulls wear blue, you see, and Nomads go for red. If they spot a child out 'flying colors,' it doesn't matter if he's in a gang or not. He could be playing in the Little League, for all these bastards care. They come around and shoot him for the color of his shirt or baseball cap."

"Both gangs are dealing crack?"

"Around the clock. A fair percentage of their customers are white. We see them coming into the Point in BMWs and Mercedes, shit and money changing hands. The cops are always somewhere else. We call, and by the time they come around, the action's moved a couple of blocks away. They can't find anything, or when they do, it's juveniles. You ever listen to the judges and the lawyers talk about a juvenile in custody?"

"Can't say I have."

"It's like a different world. The rules just don't apply. Oh, maybe if you've got a triggerman who's sixteen, seventeen years old, and they can catch him with a smoking gun. The rest of them, forget about it. Ninety, ninety-five percent pull down probation, and a handful get vacations with the California Youth Authority. A month or two at camp, and they're right back on the streets and selling shit again. That's why the gangs use minors—what they call the 'peewees'—for a great part of their dirty work."

"So you involved yourself because the system doesn't work," Bolan said.

"That's right. A few of us got sick and tired of hearing the machine guns every weekend, seeing children stretched out in the street. We talked to the police, and they came back with forty-seven reasons why there's nothing they can do. We went to city council meetings, and the council promised they'd 'look into things.' I'll give them this, they damn near passed an ordinance against the gangs, but then the civil liberties people jumped in, threatening to sue the city if they tried to punish 'children' for associating with their 'friends.' That's when I got Bill Phillips on the line.''

The name took Bolan back. A onetime comrade in the Asian hellgrounds, Phillips had been working as a San Francisco cop the first time Bolan had clashed with Northern California Mafia. He'd retired a short time later, done a turn in law school, and the last that Bolan had heard he'd been working for a well placed California congressman in Washington.

Bill Phillips also happened to be black, a product of the Point and one fine human being in the bargain. It was no great leap for Bolan to decide that Souders's call to Phillips had, in turn, produced a call to Justice, hence the contact with Brognola and a summons for the Executioner.

"I'll need whatever information you can find me on the gangs before we start," Bolan said.

"It seems to me like you've already started."

"That was their decision," Bolan stated. "I figure they were after you."

"I wouldn't argue with you there. It makes it the second time they've tried to take me out in the past three months."

"Which gang?"

"I think it was the Nomads last time. Anyway, it doesn't make much difference when they're shooting up your house."

"You understand that I'll be working independently of the police?"

"I gathered that."

"If you're uncomfortable with the approach, my best advice would be to back out while you can."

"Who says I've got a choice?"

"We all have choices."

"Look, the Point might not be much, but it's my home, all right? I've got a business there and roots in the community. My wife's been dead five years, but Corey—that's my daughter—goes to San Francisco State, prelaw. I won't be letting any two-bit teenage gangsters run me off."

"It just gets rougher," Bolan warned.

"Let's make it rough on the scum for a change. They've had their own way long enough."

"In that case," Bolan said, "why don't you tell me what you can about the gangs? Skulls first."

"Their leader's a jailbird by the name of Elroy Johnson, but they call him One Shot. That's because he's got a reputation as a cool hand with a gun, I understand. One shot from Elroy, and his enemies are history. Some of them, anyway."

"You've checked him out?"

"I've checked them all out, Mr. Blanski. No big deal, at that, the way they show up in the papers every now and then. This Johnson's twenty-six years old, or was the last I heard. He's been to prison twice on drug-related charges, and the local cops have picked him up at least a dozen times for questioning during the past two years. He walks these days because they can't find any witnesses with nerve enough to testify."

"You've worked on that?"

"The best I can. We had one widow set to tell about Elroy and a couple of his goons shooting a neighbor's house for making a complaint to the police about their dope deals on the street. Thing is, somebody torched her house a couple of days before she was supposed to testify. She didn't make it out."

"How many Skulls?"

"The cops'll tell you sixty-five. Throw in the pee-wees and some hangers-on, I make it closer to a hundred."

"Do they have some special place to congregate?"

The frown on Souders's face made Bolan wonder if his host was working on a change of heart. A moment later Souders reached back for his jacket, took a notebook from the inside pocket and handed it across. "I've been collecting names, addresses, anything I could. For Skulls and Nomads, both. You'll find it all in there."

Bolan slipped the notebook into his pocket, leaving it for later. "And the Nomads?"

"They're behind a piece of shit named Fabius Raymond. His street handle's 'Playboy,' supposed because the girls can't get enough. Myself, I don't see the attraction."

"Background?"

"Twenty-four, and he's the old man of the gang. Eleven busts the locals know about, one two-year at Vacaville for rape."

"Some playboy. What about the troops?"

"The Nomads have a few more members than the Skulls, last count. The cops say seventy, with maybe thirty, forty peewees on the fringes. That doesn't count the females, either. Both gangs treat their girls like slaves. They're good for sex and running errands, maybe carrying the hardware when their big, strong men don't want to catch the heat. I've seen them knock a girl down on the street for saying she was hungry."

"Are the girls involved in business that you know of?"

Souders shook his head. "I could be wrong, of course. Some of them trick from time to time, but that's about the size of it. I don't believe the gangs would ever trust them dealing shit.''

"You don't have photographs by any chance?"

"We haven't needed any up to now."

The warrior shrugged it off, already planning different angles of attack. "No sweat."

"What happens now?"

"You're better off not knowing," Bolan replied.

"Now *that* sounds like the cops."

"You have your differences with the police."

"They can't decide if I'm a crackpot or a vigilante, if the truth be told." The bitterness was back in Souders's voice. "They don't like a civilian—much less *black* civilians—breathing down their neck and dropping hints on how they ought to do their job. It makes them nervous. You understand?"

"I've been there."

"When the Nomads sprayed my house, one of the detectives asked me if I was happy now for all the trouble I'd been stirring up. Like it was *me,* out selling shit to children in the schoolyard, shooting people on the street."

"You strike me as an honest man," the warrior said, "so I'll be honest in return. I still don't know you well enough to trust you with my life. From here on everything I do is need-to-know. I try to minimize potential leaks whenever possible."

A flash of anger shone in the black man's eyes. "You think I'm talking to the gangs?"

"I didn't say that. But you might be, and you wouldn't even have to know it."

"Say again?"

"These gangs can't operate without intelligence, connections on the street that keep them briefed about their enemies. It's not unheard of for a leak to come from the police department...or from a concerned community association, either.''

"I can't believe anybody in the group would sell us out. They've worked too hard and lost too much to go that route.''

"They wouldn't have to," Bolan said. "A loose word here and there is all it takes. The Skulls and Nomads all have friends and relatives. Unless they're deaf and blind they can't help picking up some information now and then.''

"Well, damn.''

"And there's the matter of police again.''

"How's that?''

"When things start shaking, I'd expect they'll be around to chat to find out what you know about the fireworks, just in case. I've never seen you try to con a cop, but I'll feel better if you don't have anything to share.''

"I know your name already." Bolan's smile came back at him, and Souders shook his head. "I guess I'm in it now," the man said.

"I'm hoping I can leave you out," the Executioner replied. "I'll be in touch by telephone if it begins to look like you can help me. Otherwise, the best thing you can do is just forget we ever met.''

"That won't be easy. You mind me asking something?''

"That all depends.''

"What are you really?''

"Does it matter?''

Souders thought about it for a moment and finally shook his head. "I guess not when you're fighting for your life.''

"It would be helpful if you had someplace to stay for the next few days in case the shooters make another try."

"I'll be at work, or else at home. There's no point doing this at all if I just let them run me off."

"Your call. You have to live with it."

"I'll watch my back, no sweat. The Delta hasn't been that long ago that I've forgotten everything."

"You pulled a tour in Vietnam?"

"It's ancient history. I'm not that crazy vet you're always seeing on the tube."

"Okay."

Outside they stood together on the sidewalk. Souders shook his hand and said, "I hope you know your business, Mr. Blanski."

"So do I."

The notebook in his pockets gave him names, addresses, somewhere he could start, but Bolan needed more. A trip downtown, for instance, just to get things started on the proper track.

Check that.

The action had already started. He was rolling now, with no escape hatch if he felt like bailing out. The war was on, and it would soon be heating up.

But first he had to have a word with the police.

3

San Francisco Hall of Justice occupied a full block of Bryant Street downtown between Seventh and Harriet. The parking lot reserved for visitors was fenced and monitored around the clock by uniforms and television cameras.

Inside, the age of urban terrorism had achieved a compromise of sorts with classic architecture. Marble stairs and works of art were still in evidence, but some of their effect was dimmed by warning signs, armed guards and metal detectors. The desk sergeant who greeted you on arrival at police headquarters was secured behind a wall of armored glass designed to fend off point-blank Magnum rounds. A bomb might do the job, but not before the man had a chance to reach the Uzi or the riot shotgun mounted underneath the counter at his knee.

The sergeant studied Bolan's Washington ID, made notes and offered him directions to the third-floor offices of the Gang Intervention Unit, Lieutenant Earl Weathers commanding. A buzzer got him through the outer door. Bolan checked his side arm—a snubby .38, selected for the occasion to avoid controversy—and accepted a plastic clip-on visitor's tag before he made his way to the elevators.

Upstairs, the uniforms gave way to suits and ties, a number of detectives ambling around the hallways with their jackets off and hardware on display. Nobody gave the visitor a second glance, assuming from the pass attached to his lapel that he belonged.

Gang Intervention had a corner of the third floor to itself, about the size of two small offices combined. The door was open, and the warrior had a glimpse of filing cabinets. The walls were covered high and low with photographs—of bodies, graffiti, weapons, vehicles and mug shots—plus a huge map of the city, with the different turfs marked off in colored ink.

"Can I help you?" A black man with his sleeves rolled up moved toward him on his right, carrying a bundle of manila folders in his hand. He wore a stainless-steel Smith & Wesson automatic on his hip in a high-ride holster built for speed. The plastic surgeon who'd tried to cover up the gash along his jawline could take credit for a fairly decent job. The ancient knife wound barely showed at all.

Bolan flashed the ID. "I'm looking for Lieutenant Weathers."

"In the flesh. I thought I knew the local Justice guys."

"I'm in from Washington," the Executioner replied, "Division of Juvenile Justice and Delinquency Control."

"The name game," Weathers said. "They pay somebody by the word to think those up?"

"I wouldn't be surprised."

"My pew's back here if you want to take a load off."

Bolan followed the lieutenant to a corner by the window, settling in a plastic chair across the desk from Weathers.

"What brings you west?"

"We're looking into gang activity across the country," Bolan said, "a general survey in advance of legislation. I'll be heading for Los Angeles next week, but we've been hearing things from San Francisco, too."

"I wouldn't be surprised."

"The Skulls and Savage Nomads, is it?"

Weathers nodded. "They're the worst of twenty-seven gangs we're tracking at the moment. Understand, we've also got Hispanic gangs in town, a couple of Asian cliques that do their thing in Chinatown. The white boys call themselves the Stoners. Most of them would rather snort cocaine than sell it, but they're catching on."

"To tell the truth, my people have been starting out from scratch on this. Some of them still hear 'gang' and think about James Dean."

"I know the feeling," Weathers said. "I've got a few years left before I pull the pin myself and I can still remember when the street gangs used to duke it out or fight with switchblades, maybe use a homemade zip gun now and then. Some neighborhoods these days are like Beirut. They're packing anything you can think."

"We're interested in fresh prescriptions from the officers who know this problem best. What kind of progress are you making?"

"Progress?" Weathers almost seemed amused. "It seems to me I've heard the term. We just don't use it much."

"That bad?"

"We're not on par with L.A. yet, thank God, but we've been gaining on them. When the Skulls and Nomads get together, man, it's hell on wheels."

"I understand you've got your hands full, but the brass is after me to bring home charts and photographs, if they're available. You know the kind of thing they like to see."

"The family tree approach?"

"Exactly."

"That's no problem. We've got mug shots out the ass, and we keep books on all the major gangs. You want some photocopies, I'll gct a secretary on it. Maybe fifteen, twenty minutes. For the prints..."

"No problem. Copies should be fine. If someone on the Hill wants color blowups, they can get in touch through channels."

"Fair enough. How long you plan to be in town?"

"Not long," the Executioner replied. "I'm really on the fly."

"It must be nice to get away from time to time."

"That's what I hear."

"Well, if there's anything I can do to help out while you're here..."

"You've done it," Bolan told him, shaking hands. And he meant it.

When he left the Hall of Justice thirty-seven minutes later, he was carrying a fat manila envelope containing photographs and names for both the Skulls and Savage Nomads, with intelligence on their connections to the local dealers and suppliers from Los Angeles. The two-page list of vehicles and license numbers was a bonus that, with any luck at all, would help him spot potential tails.

Step one: identify the enemy.

The Skulls and Savage Nomads didn't know it, but they were strictly amateurs where rumbling was concerned. They were about to take a lesson from the master.

Starting now.

THE YOUNG MAN KNOWN as Devo lit a cigarette, inhaling deeply as he watched the ships glide past on San Francisco Bay. Sometimes the tramps and tankers looked like models, close enough to touch, but Devo knew they were a world apart, and he'd never bridge the gap.

One Saturday about a year ago he'd accompanied a dozen brother Nomads on the boat ride out to Alcatraz. The water had made him queasy, but he'd gotten a kick from checking out the ancient cell blocks, cracking wise about the old-time rule of silence for inmates who were dead and gone by now. Some kind of ancient history that was from days before the Man had begun to lose his grip.

It was a new day now with young bloods like himself in charge or getting there. Another year or two and you could forget the Mafia, whatever. When you mentioned someone selling shit in San Francisco, it would be the Savage Nomads all the way.

Of course, there was some nasty business to be settled first between the Nomads and the Skulls. When that was done, the other half-assed gangs would either fall in line or they'd be eliminated one by one.

Survival of the fittest, fucking A.

This afternoon the run was strictly business, picking up supplies. If Devo had his way, they'd have had their shit delivered to the Point instead of meeting some guy off the boat. But that was Playboy's call. The last thing anybody with a brain between his ears would ever do was question Playboy's orders where money was concerned.

The guy they were supposed to meet was a chicano from Los Angeles or San Diego. Devo wasn't sure which. He'd be bringing in a suitcase full of shit for them to cut a couple of dozen times before they sold it on the street. He was supposed to be alone, but you could never tell, so Devo had a couple of the brothers with him. X-ray was riding shotgun, literally with a sawed-off 12-gauge in his lap, and Pluto sat in the back seat with an Uzi and the cash.

"Dude's late," X-ray said glancing at the Rolex watch he'd lifted off a honkie businessman they'd robbed last month.

"He'll get here, cuz."

"I don't like waitin'," Pluto chimed in. "Suppose the pigs come by and we be sittin' here with all this iron?"

"The pigs ain't got no cause for roustin' us," Devo replied, watching yet another ship glide past.

"Since when they need any cause?"

"You worry too damn much."

The truth was, Devo didn't like the waiting, either, but they had no choice. When Playboy sent you out to get the weekly shipment, you shut up and did as you were told. Returning empty-handed would be tantamount to suicide.

You had to think about the gang as family, and realize that any risk you took on the family's behalf was worth the trouble if it served the greater whole. The night they'd jumped him in, when Devo had to fight his choice of Savage Nomads three on one as an initiation rite, he'd known it would be this way. He was a soldier now, and soldiers followed orders even to the death.

Along the way you had the benefits of brotherhood, sex and ready cash, provided you had balls enough to go the distance for your family. If anybody let the Nomads down, then Devo meant to be the first in line to kick some ass.

"That him?"

He followed X-ray's pointing finger toward the far end of the pier and saw a figure moving toward them with a bulky suitcase in one hand. He looked Hispanic, and his free hand was tucked inside the pocket of his nylon jacket, maybe wrapped around a piece. "Could be. Y'all keep a lookout now."

The gofer seemed to recognize their wheels, and he was making for the car with all deliberate speed. There were supposed to be three dozen kilo bags of flake inside the suitcase, and it would be Devo's job to make the count before the money changed hands.

"Hang in."

"I'm hangin', cuz."

He stepped out of the car, his pistol in his waistband. He wore his red plaid jacket unbuttoned, with his baseball cap reversed. A walking fashion plate, gangbanger style.

The mule was thirty yards away and closing fast when something happened. Devo didn't catch it right away, heard only the engine sound and screech of tires. Some clumsy bastard deciding he couldn't beat the traffic light. No sweat.

Before Devo had a chance to glance around he saw the gofer looking off in the direction of the noise and blinking, something close to panic in his eyes. Next thing his head exploded like a melon on the chopping block, and he went down, a boneless rag doll flopping on the pavement.

Devo heard a shout of warning from the car before he turned and saw the shooter sighting through the driver's window of a compact vehicle. He hadn't heard the shot because the Uzi was fitted with a silencer, its muzzle looking like a goddamn railroad tunnel.

He tried to dodge, already groping for his weapon, and the bullet caught him beneath the collarbone. Its impact spun him around once and dumped him onto the blacktop where he gasped from the pain and cursed as his gun slid out of reach.

Pluto's return fire was off the mark. The shooter squeezed off four quick rounds and canceled out two of the gang members before they could wonder what the hell was going down.

Some kind of rip-off, Devo reasoned, on his own now. His eyes swam in and out of focus, but it hardly mattered. With the ski mask and the gloves he couldn't tell enough about the shooter to provide a thumbnail sketch. The license plate was out of range and out of sight before the bleeding Nomad realized he was still alive.

Pigs coming, damn it, and he couldn't even find the strength to crawl away before they got there. Money in the car and cocaine in the suitcase. How the hell was he supposed to beat a rap like that, assuming he survived?

One thing at least. He didn't need the shooter's name to know who had put him on the street. The Skulls had gone too far this time, and Playboy would be taking care of business once he got the word.

THE CRACK HOUSE WAS an eyesore on Arieta, due east of McLaren Park. Like others of its type, it was officially abandoned and unoccupied. The legal owners had decamped three years ago, and while the property was theoretically available for purchase, there were no signs in the yard, no realtors in the city stupid enough to bring prospective customers around.

The neighborhood itself still had some pride, but various appeals to the police had failed to shut down the crack house. When things got rowdier than usual, a squad car might swing by and give the Skulls a chance to scatter. A search would turn up nothing but the empty rooms, graffiti, condoms scattered in among the beer cans, junk food wrappers and assorted other trash.

The house attracted many visitors. Most came to purchase drugs from the attendant Skulls, who drifted in and out with their supplies between the visits by police. Some came to party, and the neighbors were beginning to accommodate their schedule, learning from experience that nuisance calls about the noise meant payback in the form of vandalism, beatings or a sudden fire.

From time to time there would be a hostile face among the visitors. A couple of the Savage Nomads would cruise by to check out the action perhaps and fire a few stray shots to keep the Skulls from feeling too secure. It was a part of doing business in the city, and for nearby residents who lived in constant fear of flying bullets, sometimes it meant sleeping on the floor with makeshift weapons close at hand.

The night he closed the crack house Bolan parked a half block down and watched the traffic for a moment, counting vehicles and dealers in the yard. Within five minutes he witnessed six transactions, dope and money changing hands in daylight in the middle of a San Francisco residential neighborhood.

Enough.

He slipped on the ski mask, remembering to daub black camou paint around his eyes before he slipped his hands into the skintight gloves. The rest of his body was covered, from the turtleneck down to the high-top combat boots he wore. It might not be enough to make survivors think he was a black man, but it would give them cause to wonder. He was counting on the predator's inherent paranoia for the rest.

A couple of the dealers saw him coming, grenades and handguns swinging on the harness that he wore. They bolted for the house, abandoning their latest customer at curbside, and the college type in his Toyota needed only one glimpse of the Executioner before he burned rubber out of there.

The warrior had the Uzi primed and ready by the time he reached the yard, a flicker of the curtains at a broad front window all he needed to direct a burst in that direction. Someone started cursing on the inside of the house as Parabellum bullets raked the walls and ceiling, bringing down a rain of plaster dust.

He palmed a fragmentation grenade, released the safety pin and pitched the bomb through the shattered window, waiting for the blast before he pressed ahead. The cursing was replaced by screams and cries of panic, survivors bailing out the back or the windows as Bolan hit the front door with a flying kick and followed through.

Immediately on his left two guys were down, a third on hands and knees with fresh blood spilling from his face. The Skull was reaching for a weapon on the floor when Bolan stroked the Uzi's trigger lightly, half a dozen rounds on target, pummeling the dead gang member over onto his back.

The warrior made his way from room to room, alert to any hint of danger, but the place was vacant now. He dropped the first incendiary in what used to be a bedroom, backing out before the fuse ran down and white-hot thermite sprayed the walls and ignited everything it touched. A second can was left in the living room, the empty shell engulfed in flame and burning brightly by the time he reached the curb.

One crack house out of business. The warrior spotted a couple of the neighbors coming out to watch as he retreated toward his car. They viewed the conflagration with a kind of wonder, basking in reflected heat and smiling. The fire had been a long time coming, but it seemed to thaw their souls.

The Executioner had no illusion that the destruction of a single crack house—or a hundred houses—would prevent the gangs from moving drugs. It was enough for now to plant the seeds of paranoia with his enemies and let them sprout.

Step two was isolation of the enemy, no easy task when you were fighting on an urban battlefield. Sometimes the best you could do was to turn one faction on another, play upon their natural distrust and fan the sparks of mutual suspicion into roaring flames.

With any luck at all the Skulls and Nomads would soon help Bolan to do his job. But he wasn't about to sit and wait.

Not while he still had calls to make.

4

Some mornings Captain Barney Gibson wondered if God disliked him with a vengeance, or if all the shit he had to wade through on his job was mere coincidence. On other days, like this one, he didn't have to ask.

Gibson had eleven months to go before retirement, thirty years behind a badge in San Francisco, and he figured he'd seen it all—basic thieves and smugglers, con men, pimps and hookers, contract killers, right on down the line to psycho hackers and Satanic cults. Name the felony of choice, and Barney Gibson could recount at least one case from personal experience to fit the bill. It stood to reason that with twenty-nine years on the job he wasn't easily disgusted or surprised.

But he was getting tired, and the job was getting on his nerves. It showed up in his yearly physical with signs of stress and blood pressure edging toward the danger zone. Gibson knew his doctor would relax a little once he finally pulled the pin.

Next year.

It seemed like something in a dream, the way kids fantasize about leaving home or graduating from high school, feeling all the time as if the anticipated day would never come.

It wasn't that he craved the "good old days," by any means. Police work rubbed your nose in blood and filth regardless of the year you started on the job, but he couldn't deny that things were getting worse out there. A few years back, somebody mentioned gang wars and he thought about Sicilians, armored limousines and going to the mattresses. It was tradition, understood by everybody, and the bastards mostly killed their own. Some even said it was a public service, thinning out the herd.

These days the casualties were different, and it went beyond the fact of ethnic background, race or residence. Today an urban gang war meant machine-gun fire in schoolyards, children cut down in convenience stores or in their homes. With modern youth gangs shooters lacked the skill or social conscience to eliminate their victims tidily. If spotters made their target in a crowd of ten or fifteen teenage innocents, the options narrowed down to one—shoot 'em all, and let the Man sort it out.

It was a sorry day, Gibson decided, when he filed the papers for a transfer into Homicide. Considered the elite by many officers, it meant that he confronted violent death each day without the more or less benign diversion of a robbery or hijack case to let him catch his breath.

Lately Gibson had a whole new rash of murders on his plate. The Skulls and Savage Nomads were apparently progressing from sporadic sniping incidents to full-scale slaughter, dropping Gibson in the middle of a case Gang Intervention would have handled otherwise. He'd already viewed the crime scenes—blood and brains on pavement, smell of roasting flesh—and he was rolling toward an interview with a civilian who reportedly had nursed a hard-on for the gangs these past two years.

"I don't know what you'll get from this guy," Weathers had advised him, "but it's worth a shot. He calls us every week or two with some complaint about the gangs, and he's been organizing neighbors."

Great. The last thing Gibson needed in his city at the moment was a goddamn righteous vigilante helping to police the streets. That kind of "help" was no damn help at all. But if the guy had any solid information on the killings it would be another story. Either way, the captain told himself, he was obliged to check it out.

The house on Cochrane Street was small and well kept, a decent place for Hunters Point. His driver parked out front and waited in the car to man the radio and make sure no one stripped the vehicle while Gibson did his interview. The doorbell worked, and in another moment he heard footsteps coming closer, someone opening the dead-bolt latch.

He pegged the girl—make that "young woman"—somewhere in her early twenties.

"Yes?"

He made a pass with the credentials, giving her time to read them through the screen.

"I'm here to speak with Mr. Vernon Souders," Gibson told her. "He's expecting me, I think."

Reluctantly she opened the screen. "Come in."

She double-locked the door and led him to a living room that had to rank among the cleanest Gibson had ever seen. The place was getting on in years, of course, but you could tell without a second glance that these were people who took pride in where they lived, the kind who wouldn't let a bunch of teenage assholes run them off without a fight.

Perhaps without a killing?

"Father, this is Captain Gibson. Captain, my father."

Having made her introducions, the young lady sought a neutral corner, settling in an easy chair directly opposite the couch. Souders's grip was firm and dry, his gaze direct, unflinching. "Won't you please sit down?"

With Souders on the couch, that left a deep recliner for Gibson, and he took it, feeling somewhat like a midget as he sank back in the deep upholstery.

"Nice place you've got here."

"Thank you. Would you like some coffee?"

"No thanks."

"Well, then."

"As I informed you on the telephone, we've had some action with the Skulls and Nomads off and on today."

"The shootings, yes. I heard."

Was that a glimmer of discomfort in the eyes? Too soon to tell.

"Gang Intervention filled me in on some of your attempts to keep the gangs from spreading, and I was concerned about the possibility that you might have some information on the day's events."

"You mean to say that I might be involved."

"I didn't say that, Mr. Souders."

"Captain." The young woman interrupting him, a stern expression on her face. "Do you have any reason to suspect my father of these crimes?"

"No, ma'am." Not yet, he felt like adding, but he kept it to himself.

"The street gangs in this city murder one another every day. It must be clear to the police what's happening, and yet you still can't make a dent in their activities."

He forced a smile. "I'll bet you're still in college, right?"

"Prelaw at San Francisco State."

"Then you're acquainted with the Bill of Rights. As much as I might like to lock up the Skulls and Nomads for breathing God's clean air, I have to make a case and push it through the system, just like everybody else."

"I'm not concerned with how they breathe," Vernon Souders said. "We're discussing willful murder, robbery and rape, illegal drug transactions taking place in daylight on the public streets. An amateur photographer could document narcotics cases left and right in Hunters Point. I have some videocassettes myself."

"I understand there was a shooting here not long ago."

Fresh paint behind the couch covered up the work of patching bullet holes. If Gibson checked the putty on the windows, he'd bet that it was relatively new.

"That's right."

"You've got some enemies out there."

"Some friends, as well."

"None of them leaning toward revenge, by any chance?"

"Speak plainly, Captain. I'm a busy man."

"Okay. A group like yours gets organized to save the neighborhood from crime. You work within the system, but it's full of holes. The bad guys keep on slipping through, and the police aren't always johnny on the spot."

"To put it mildly," the young woman interjected, frowning.

"Time goes by, and maybe one of your associates decides he ought to pay the little bastards back. The cops can't do a job, so bring back the good old San Francisco vigilantes for a while."

Once more something flickered in the eyes before the black man spoke. It could be simple irritation, or...

"I'm sorry, Captain, but I have no information that would help you. I don't espouse a vigilante line, by any means. I simply urge legitimate authorities to do their job."

"You've been in touch with Washington. I understand."

Souders stiffened, but his voice was calm as he replied. "I've had no answer, and I frankly don't expect one. It appears the federal agencies are no more interested in rampant homicide and drugs than San Francisco's finest."

Gibson felt the angry color rising in his cheeks and tried to calm himself. "We're interested, all right. The problem is, we never seem to find a witness who'll agree to testify. A couple dozen of your neighbors watch a murder going down, and no one sees a thing. That's just a tad peculiar, don't you think, considering this great concern you talk about?"

"That isn't fair," the woman snapped. "These people have been living with the gangs for years. They're terrified of retribution, and they know your department won't protect them if they testify."

"We haven't had the chance so far. I'd like to try."

"I'll see what I can do," Souders told him.

"Wonderful. And, in the meantime, if your sources turn up anything..."

"I don't have 'sources,' Captain. Those I work with are my friends."

"Whatever." Gibson rose and passed a business card to the man. "If your *friends* come up with anything, it wouldn't hurt to drop a coin."

The woman saw him off without goodbyes, and Gibson stalked back to the waiting car. He couldn't put a finger on the feeling, and his gut was telling him Souders had some deeper knowledge of the case than he was letting on. A name perhaps, or maybe just an educated hunch.

"How was it?" his driver asked.

"Waste of time," the captain replied.

So far.

IT WAS HER FATHER'S attitude that puzzled Corey Souders most of all. In other confrontations with police he'd been more assertive, righteous indignation ringing in his every word. This afternoon with Captain Gibson he was more reserved, appearing ill at ease.

Almost as if he'd been holding something back.

It was ridiculous, of course. What could her father know about the sudden rash of gang-related homicides?

She found him in the kitchen, making coffee.

"Daddy, can we talk a minute?" She reserved the affectionate address for their private moments, and would never have used it in front of the captain.

"Sure we can. What's on your mind?"

"I feel a little funny...."

"There's no reason why you should. I thought we understood each other."

"Right, okay." The understanding dated from before her mother's death. Full honesty, and no hard feelings afterward. "When you were talking to the captain, well, it felt as if you were holding something back."

"Such as?"

She frowned. "If I knew that, I guess I wouldn't have to ask."

"You think I have some knowledge of the shootings that I didn't share?"

"I know you were uncomfortable."

"The man was sitting there, accusing me of setting up a vigilante murder ring. I didn't like the sound of that."

"No reason why you should. But I was thinking of the way you looked when he was asking you about your contact with the federal government."

Her father turned away to check the coffee's progress. "Oh? And how, exactly, did I look?"

"Like there was something more you could have said."

"You mean, like I was lying."

"Dad—"

"In fact, you're right." He turned to face her, putting on a frown. "I didn't tell the captain everything."

She felt a sudden quickening inside herself, as if piano wires were being tightened in her chest.

"I'm listening."

"I told him there was no response from Washington," her father said. "That wasn't true. In fact, an agent spoke to me this morning."

"And?"

"They might be starting an investigation of the local gangs, some kind of interstate conspiracy or some such. If they want to get in touch with the police, I leave that up to them."

"Is it supposed to be a secret?"

"Corey, I've been calling the police with every scrap of information I could lay my hands on for the past two years with no result. We might not get relief from Washington, either, but at least they're listening. I don't intend to stir things up by pitting the police against the federal government. You know the way they hassle over jurisdiction all the time."

"That's all?"

"What else?"

She forced a smile and shook her head, uneasy with the feeling in her gut. It was the first time in her life that she had reason to mistrust her father's word, but all the signs were there. She knew he was holding back some bit of information, something he feared might worry her if it was shared.

There seemed to be no point in grilling him and stirring up an argument, especially when she was running late for class, but Corey was determined not to let it go. If necessary, she'd do some snooping on her own and try to find out what the federal men were up to and how her father was involved.

Above all else she didn't want him threatened, harmed or jeopardized in any way. She understood his quiet courage and determination to repulse the gangs from Hunters Point, and she admired him for the stand he'd taken...to a point. The flip side of her understanding was a brooding fear of losing the only parent she had left.

The first attempt to kill her father had been bad enough, but she wasn't prepared to live that nightmare on a daily basis, going on and on until some worthless piece of human trash got lucky on a drive-by and her world was torn apart.

No, thank you.

If Corey had to get involved, so be it. It was worth the risk, and she'd hate herself if something happened while she sat around and took no action of her own.

"You want some coffee, hon?"

She tried on her sweetest smile for size. "I wouldn't mind."

THE "CLUBHOUSE" of the Savage Nomads was a small apartment complex the gang had overrun, evicting lawful tenants through a campaign of harassment, moving in and paying partial rent the first two months before sending a scouting party to the landlord's home to let him know he should feel grateful his bones and family were still intact.

It did the trick.

These days the compound was an armed encampment, and police had managed to avoid a raid. With no complaint on file from the established owner there was little they could do. Nuisance calls from neighbors simply weren't worth the risk of a protracted firefight when the problem was illegal parking or a noisy stereo.

An ethnic breakdown of the low-rent neighborhood would have revealed that it was ninety-two percent nonwhite with about fifteen percent of those inhabitants recorded as Hispanic. Going in, the Executioner was well aware he'd have to "pass" before he could complete his work, and he fell back upon role camouflage to do the trick.

He bagged the van, belonging to an air-conditioning repair shop, from the back of a fast-food restaurant. The coveralls were standard-issue janitorial attire with somebody else's name embroidered on the chest. The Marlin lever-action .444 Magnum rifle fitted inside his toolbox after being broken down.

No one gave him a second glance at the apartment complex three doors down, across the street from where the Savage Nomads made their home. He found the service stairs and gambled that the air-conditioning compressor units would be mounted on the roof. He encountered no resistance on the rooftop and took his time assembling the Marlin, slotting rounds into the magazine and peering through the twenty-power sight.

The Executioner had never shot fish in a barrel, but he was familiar with the expression. From a hundred yards the scope made his targets close to life-size as the cross hairs settled first on one face, then another. Playboy Raymond made a brief appearance at a window, but the warrior let him go. He'd be needing Playboy for a while if he intended to succeed with his projected strategy.

The other Nomads were expendable, however, and he started looking for a likely place to start.

Perhaps the pool.

A lack of maintenance had left it filthy, more a breeding ground for insects than a place for recreation, but the rulers of the complex lounged around the deck regardless, sipping beer and wine, a couple of them passing joints from hand to hand. The female hangers-on were much in evidence intent on catering to every whim of their lords and masters without complaint.

He picked a surly face at random, let it fill the scope and thumbed back the Marlin's hammer.

It was high time these predators were educated in the cost of war.

His finger tightencd on the trigger.

5

"You *saw* the man?"

For Elroy "One Shot" Johnson it was all that he could do to keep from picking up a gun and finishing off the son of a bitch who stood in front of him. The brother's name was Zero, and his odds of living through the night were less than that unless he managed to explain how he'd let some crazy bastard trash the crack house on Arleta Avenue.

"We all four saw him," Zero answered, staring at his bedroom slippers as he spoke.

"Four?"

"There was High Top, Boner, Spoke and me."

A recitation of the dead.

"I'm lookin' at the only one who walked away," the leader of the Skulls replied. "You want to tell me why that is?"

"We saw this crazy fucker comin' down Arleta, walkin' with a fuckin' Uzi, and we all ran back inside the house, okay? The way he dressed up like a soldier with a fuckin' ski mask on, we couldn't tell if he was DEA or what, you know? Spoke handed me the bag of shit and told me I should haul ass out the back, then wait and see what was goin' down."

"I'm listening."

"I did like I was told, okay? Next thing I hear is shootin', like the Uzi gettin' down, and then some kind of an explosion from the house. I started back inside, but then the fuckin' place was all on fire, like when you drop a match in fuckin' gasoline. I never seen a place go up like that."

"So then you ran away?"

Zero looked confused.

"Hell, yes, I ran away. What was I supposed to do? I'm standin' there with six or seven pounds of rock. You think I oughta hang around and give it to the man?"

"You left your brothers," One Shot told him, glaring.

"They was *dead,* I'm tellin' you. If you'd seen that place, you wouldn't have to ask was they alive."

"So where's the rock?"

Another downward shift of Zero's eyes. "Well, see, I passed a couple of pigmobiles when I was leavin', all lit up and sirens goin'. I thought they was going to gaffle me up, so, well, I dropped it in a garbage can."

"You fucking stupid piece of shit."

"I done the best I could."

"Three brothers die to give you time, and then you throw the fucking rock *away?* What kind of best is that, I want to know?"

"The fuckin' pigs was everywhere, okay? I didn't want to take no fall for holdin' major weight, especially with the brothers lyin' back there two, three blocks away. First thing I know, they be accusin' *me* of smokin' out the place."

"It crossed my mind," One Shot said, watching Zero squirm, "except I figure you don't got the balls."

The younger man said nothing, simply stood there and took it. He obviously knew he was lucky just to be alive.

"Here's what you do," One Shot instructed him, the tone of his voice allowing no debate. "From now on everything you move, you kick back half until you pay back double the expense of what you threw away. Sound fair to you?"

"I guess."

"Say what?"

"It's fair."

"That's settled then. Man owes the family, he pays his debts. Next thing we got to think about is who took down our fuckin' house. Same piece of shit that bitched our hit on the old man, I wouldn't be surprised."

It was the worst day One Shot Johnson could remember since the last time he'd gone sailing on parole. The move on Vernon Souders should have been a milk run, tag and shag, but he had four men dead behind that piece of work, and no one could explain to him how Souders had walked away.

The old man was a loudmouth, sure, and there was word around the street that he'd been some kind of hero back in Vietnam a hundred years ago, but that was ancient history. The times that he'd faced down Skulls or Nomads in the past, he never tried to muscle anybody, telling them instead how he was talking to the feds, the DA's office, this and that. Of course, he might have started packing heat these days, since Playboy Raymond's people tried to waste him at his house. Too many psychos on the streets these days for you to second-guess a guy like that.

One thing, for sure, Johnson knew the old man didn't burn the crack house on Arleta. Even if he used a piece in self-defense and had the luck to drop four brothers in a pile, it didn't mean he was dressing up like GI Joe and wiping houses off the map.

That sounded more like Playboy Raymond and the Nomads.

If nothing else, it marked a new phase in the war between the city's leading gangs. So far the Skulls and Nomads had been sniping at each other, pulling drivebys, maybe ripping off a shipment when they had the chance. One Shot had sent some people by the Nomad compound once to waste a couple of their cars outside, and that was fun. More to the point, it was *expected*.

This gig on Arleta now was something else.

Some kind of balls that took to smoke a crack house out and kill three well-armed brothers in the process. All the more if Zero had it right and there was only one guy on the job. No face, what with the mask pulled down, but One Shot figured it had to be a heavy hitter from the Nomads, turning up the heat.

He sat in silence for a moment, running down the list of possible contenders for a job like that. If it was on the other foot, the fire would make him think of High Test, but the Nomads didn't have a special torch the last he heard. A big guy, Zero had said, dressed up in military clothes.

His first thought would have been for Baby Rambo, the way he loved that paramilitary shit, but he was sitting out a no-bail in the county lockup, waiting on a trial for strong-arm robbery and rape. The biggest guys the Nomads had, aside from Playboy, would be Snoops and Judo. Still...

He broke the train of thought, aware that he was taking too much time. Decisive action was the mark of leadership, and part of that was hitting back with everything you had when someone started stepping on your toes.

"The Numbnuts are asking for it this time," he proclaimed, referring to the Savage Nomads by the name preferred among their enemies. "They've gone too far."

"Right on!" A chorus from the faithful came back to reinforce his anger. Faces watched him intently, each alert for his instructions. "They want a fucking war, we'll give 'em one."

"Somebody gave 'em one already."

One Shot recognized the voice of Weed, his number two, and turned to find the young man pushing past a couple of the brothers, entering the meeting room.

"How's that?"

"It's on the pig band," Weed informed him, nodding toward the kitchen, where they kept a police scanner running off and on. "Somebody hit the Nomads at their clubhouse, long-range like. Meat wagons rolling out. I didn't catch how many dead."

A couple of the brothers started slapping hands and grinning, but they shut it off when One Shot snapped his fingers at them for silence. "Who's the shooter? Did they say?"

"He didn't stick around. If I was Playboy, I'd be thinkin' it was us."

"It should have been," somebody muttered in the back, and One Shot burned him with a glare.

"How long ago was this?" the leader of the Skulls asked Weed.

"Not long. They're rollin' on it now."

"They hit us first, then."

"Thirty, forty minutes, anyhow."

"Goddamn it, something crazy's goin' on."

"No crazy to it," Weed replied. "The Numbnuts took a shot at us, and somebody else got down on them. Coincidence."

"Like who?"

"You name it, cuz. The Rolling Sixties maybe, or the Northridge A.C.'s. Playboy and his soldiers have been crowdin' them the past few weeks."

"I ain't so sure."

"Who else?"

"If I knew that, I wouldn't ask the fucking question, would I?"

"Easy, cuz. I ain't the enemy around here."

"Okay, forget about whoever hit the Numbnuts. *They* hit *us,* and that's what matters. If we don't hit back, we might as well roll over and let 'em fuck us anytime they want."

"I heard that, bro."

"So listen up." The leader of the Skulls was back in charge. "I got a plan."

THE COPS WERE clearing out at last, and Playboy Raymond felt a measure of his cool returning as the final squad car pulled away. It had been two hours since the shit had gone down. He had three soldiers on the way to metal tables in the morgue and two others torn up bad enough that the paramedics questioned whether they'd live. Without the necessary paperwork the dicks and uniforms had sniffed around a little, taking pictures of the blood and bodies, but they couldn't search the place the way they wanted to.

Some days you had to take your hat off to the old white dudes who'd written the Bill of Rights.

"They gone?"

His number two, T-Bone, was standing at his elbow, checking out the street. A few stray neighbors stood staring toward the compound, sniffing after blood, but none of them had nerve enough to cross the street. The way it should be, right.

"All gone," Playboy said, turning back to face his second-in-command. "I heard one of 'em say they found some shells up on the roof a few doors down the other side. The motherfucker had to have a scope, no question."

"That's a new one for the Scumbags."

Normally the leader of the Savage Nomads would have laughed when T-Bone ragged the Skulls that way, but he'd lost his sense of humor when the guns went off.

"Old dog can learn himself new tricks sometimes."

"I guess."

"You don't think One Shot's good for this?"

"He probably is," T-Bone replied, "but . . ."

"But what?"

"The word came in while you were talking to the pigs about the Scumbags' crack house on Arleta."

"What about it?"

"Gone." There was an anxious look on T-Bone's face. "Somebody took it off like it was nothin'. Dynamite, they say, some shit like that. They got some people dead up there."

"Tough shit."

"Thing is, I figure One Shot has to think *we* struck the match."

"And now he's hittin' back at us for something we never did?"

"Somebody ask for my opinion, I expect that's right."

"Dumb bastard. He's connected with a world of hurt this time."

"You want to take him?"

"What the hell you think? I oughta make believe nothin' happened here?"

"I didn't say that, man."

"Then what?"

"We still don't know what happened with the morning shipment from L.A. We going to do a thing, we need to get it right first time."

"I know damn well what happened to the shipment," Playboy snapped. "The fuckin' Scumbags tried to rip us off, but one of them got trigger-happy and it fell apart. They missed the money, and the shit they came for. Add it up, that's probably why they got pissed off and hit us where we live."

"I guess that's right."

"You *know* it's right."

"So what do you want to do about it, cuz?"

"I'm thinkin'. You go check around, make sure the pigs left things alone, like they were supposed to. Anything shows missing, and I went to know about it double-quick."

"Right on."

Alone once more he tried to sort out the pieces and make them fit. The shipment first. No problem, when you thought about it. Shit like that was always going on, gangs ripping off one another whenever they could get away with it. Three-quarters of the shootings in the city had to do with crack deliveries or sales, the street gangs feuding over territory and supplies. There wasn't room in San Francisco for a hundred different outfits selling shit to whitey. Some of them would have to fall, and soon, to clear the way for those who would survive.

Right now, though, Playboy Raymond had to get his ass in gear. A leader had to lead, and that meant busting someone's chops when they came out against the family. You never let an insult pass, or it got easier the next time for your enemies to walk all over you. A little bit of that and you were history.

For Playboy Raymond there were no two ways about it. He'd built his reputation stepping on the other guy and never taking shit from anyone. When he was in the joint, a couple of the heavy-duty faggots had tried to rough him up, and he'd sent them both to the infirmary in sorry shape. Word had gotten around, and he was left alone.

It was the same thing on the streets, except you had a bigger pool of competition standing by and waiting for your guard to drop. The Skulls were number one on Playboy's list, but there were other gangs around that would be tickled pink to see him take a fall. They saw the Savage Nomads showing class and had to make it back the best they could.

Good luck.

It bothered him about the crack house on Arleta. Not that someone struck the match, by any means, but that he had no way of knowing who'd done the job. The Skulls would think it had come from him, and that was fine with Playboy if it kept them in their place. The trouble was that One Shot Johnson had a reputation to protect, and he was hitting back against the Nomads for a job they didn't even pull.

Spilt milk.

Rule was, you do with what you've got. The situation that confronted Playboy Raymond now was something he couldn't change. It made no difference that the Skulls were wrong about the crack house raid, as long as they believed the Nomads were responsible. For Raymond's part, he'd have liked to shake the banger's hand...and maybe offer him a deal to go ahead and finish off the job.

Small chance of that, the way things looked. Whoever torched the crack house was probably as hostile to the Nomads as he was to One Shot and the Skulls. Alliances between the city's gangs were rare these days when everybody wanted in on the bonanza from cocaine. Why form a partnership when you could get yourself a gun and try to grab it all?

The surest way to deal with competition was directly, whether you were in the joint or on the street. If One Shot Johnson and the Scumbags thought the Savage Nomads were an easy touch, it would be Playboy Raymond's job to teach them otherwise.

They kept their hardware in the basement of the compound mostly, where the janitor had once stored tools. Not all the hardware certainly—he wasn't stupid—but you had to have materials at hand for self-defense. As soon as T-Bone verified that everything was safe and sound, it would be time to roll.

This afternoon had been a nightmare, with bullets flying left and right and no shooter you could see, much less respond to. Playboy Raymond had been sitting in his upstairs office, getting head from Little Eva, when the shit came down. By simply turning to the window he could watch his people die, their heads exploding as if somebody had been packing fireworks in their ears.

It was a sight he wouldn't forget, a helpless feeling he couldn't shake.

Somebody had to pay for making Playboy Raymond feel as if he was less than what a righteous leader ought to be. They had to pay with everything they had, and then some. Fucking-A.

He caught a glimpse of T-Bone coming back, the high sign telling him their hardware was intact.

"I want the troops together," Playboy told him. "Round 'em up. Five minutes by the pool."

"You got it, cuz."

No shit.

He had it, and he wasn't letting go for anybody. If the Scumbags or some other gang had eyes for Playboy Raymond's territory, they'd have to kill him first and pry his cold, dead fingers off the steering wheel.

It was the only way to go.

And it was payback time.

6

Bolan took a breather after the attack on the Nomads' compound, backing off to let the action simmer while he made a call. The telephone rang half a dozen times before Vernon Souders answered, sounding edgy on the far end of the line.

"Hello?"

"You recognize my voice?"

"I do." There was another beat before he said, "I don't think we should talk right now."

"A problem with your phone?"

"It's possible."

"Okay."

He was about to cradle the receiver, write it off, when Souders asked, "Why don't I meet you somewhere?"

Something was on his mind if he was frightened of a tap but ready to run the risk of being seen in public with the Executioner.

"You have a place in mind?"

"Just north of where we met this morning there's a playground. We can go from there."

"I'll need some time," the warrior said. "Say, half an hour?"

"Fine. I've got some cleaning up to do."

"Till then."

The line went dead, and Bolan hung up. He spent a moment mulling over Souders's words and looking for a trap, but there was nothing he could put his finger on.

San Francisco was famous for its public playgrounds, forty-eight of them listed by name in the Miscellaneous index of Bolan's city map. Assuming someone had been tapping into Souders's private line, it couldn't be known which playground he intended for the meet—unless, of course, he tipped them off beforehand.

No. It made no sense by any stretch of the imagination. Even if the man was frightened or repulsed by Bolan's tactics, setting up an ambush for the man whom he'd called for help didn't appear to be his style. The Executioner believed himself to be a decent judge of character, and he was gambling on the fact that Vernon Souders wouldn't sell him out.

Due north of Candlestick would mean the Gilman Playground, and the thirty-minute ETA was roughly three times what the warrior actually required to reach the spot. He used the extra time on recon, checking out the playground and surrounding streets for vehicles or passersby who didn't fit the neighborhood. Mixed races here, but he was on alert for any of the standout "unmarked" cars police and federal agents drove, as well as any gang-type vehicles or faces on the street. He made two circuits of the block before he parked on Ingerson, waiting for Souders to appear.

He recognized the Plymouth Fury, rolling south on Giants Drive and turning into Ingerson, the stern-faced driver passing him without a sidelong glance but pointing briefly with the index finger of the hand that held the steering wheel. The Fury dwindled in the rearview mirror, fading out of sight while Bolan checked his back and flanks for any sign of enemies.

A blue Chevette drove by, with a young woman at the wheel, but otherwise the coast was clear as far as he could see.

He twisted the ignition key and drove the short half block to Giants Drive, circling the interchange and doubling back on Ingerson westbound. He kept to the speed limit, doubly alert for any sign of a tail, covering three blocks before he saw the Plymouth parked outside a convenience store at Ingerson and Hawes. He pulled in and waited for Souders to emerge with a foam cup of coffee.

Dusk was falling as the man took a seat in Bolan's vehicle.

"I think I'm clean," Souders said without preamble. "I was checking."

"So was I."

"I thought you might be after what went down this morning."

"I'm more interested in what's been happening since then."

"Police were at my house a while ago. A Captain Gibson out of Homicide."

"Barney Gibson?"

"Could have been. You know him?"

"Only by his reputation." False, but Souders hadn't called the meet to catch a seminar on Bolan's private history. "What did he want?"

"You've had a busy day. He doesn't like the bodies piling up, I guess."

"Why come to you?"

"My guess would be Gang Intervention let him have a list of names of the folks who've filed complaints against the Skulls and Nomads time and time again. I got the feeling he suspected I was heading up some kind of vigilante operation in the Point."

"And when he left?"

"I'd be a liar if I told you he was satisfied. I don't believe he knows about this morning yet, but it's on record that the gangs have tried to waste me once before."

"He thinks you're hitting back?"

"He wouldn't come right out and say so, but it's on his mind."

Bolan caught a flash of blue in the rearview mirror. Glancing up, he was surprised to see the same Chevette that had passed him on Ingerson before he'd swung to follow Souders.

Mere coincidence?

"I'll see what I can do with the police," Bolan said, intent on disengaging now. "No promises."

"Don't sweat it. If they're watching me, at least I'll stand a fifty-fifty chance of living through the next few days."

"They might be back to question you again."

"What can I say? They want to hear about the gangs, I'll talk their ears off. Otherwise I'm ignorant."

"Okay. I'll be in touch."

There was no sign of the Chevette as Souders pulled away, no tail on Bolan as he left the parking lot a moment later, driving west to Third Street, turning north from there.

So he'd seen the same young woman and her car on two occasions, driving back and forth on Ingerson. So what? She missed the address she was looking for, or else her errand was a snap. It happened all the time....

He put the problem out of mind and concentrated on a more immediate concern—one Barney Gibson, still in harness after all this time, and working Homicide. The captain had been heading up the Harbor Detail when their paths crossed last and they'd forged a loose alliance in a common cause.

Already looking for a pay phone, Bolan wondered whether there was any chance of history repeating, lightning striking twice. If nothing else, he might be able to distract some heat from Souders, if he got in touch.

It was time to make a call for old times' sake.

ANOTHER GODFORSAKEN DAY that seemed to last forever, bodies piling up, no end in sight. The burning in his stomach might not be an ulcer, but Barney Gibson thought he'd earned one during his years of rubbing shoulders with the worst scum the city could produce.

At least he wasn't working in Los Angeles. For every gang or psycho killer working San Francisco, there would be at least a dozen in L.A. It helped him put things in perspective when he thought about it that way, but the burning in his stomach didn't ease.

He'd spent the day standing over bodies, running here and there to keep up with the rash of homicide reports. They were creeping up on twenty dead in gang-related incidents since morning, and he wouldn't bet against a few more shootings by the time midnight rolled around.

He checked the calendar. No moon to speak of, and another theory bit the dust. Full moons brought out the worst in people, sometimes doubling or even tripling reports of violent crime, but there was no way he could put the blame on Mother Nature this time. Something was cooking on the streets perhaps, but Weathers down at GIU had pumped his best informants all day long, and they were coming up with squat.

A yellow legal pad on his desk was filled with scribblings, his attempt to find a pattern in the crimes that made some sense. On one side of the sheet he'd done a rough chronology, beginning with the massacre of four young Skulls at Bay View Park. From there it gathered steam—three Nomads and a South American supplier gunned down on the waterfront; the crack house on Arleta up in flames; a sniper blasting at the Nomads' clubhouse.

It went back and forth, a deadly give-and-take with the appearance of a classic gang war, but the sources tapped by Weathers indicated nothing in the wind that would have sparked this kind of murder marathon. It was a given that the Skulls and Nomads hated each other, living in a constant state of war, but random drive-bys didn't translate into what had happened in the past eight hours.

Snipers.

Running down the inventory, Gibson found a listing for the .444 Magnum cartridges recovered by Forensics. Five rounds, quick and clean.

The telephone rang, and Gibson lifted the receiver reluctantly. No matter who was on the line it had to be bad news.

"Hello?"

"How you are, Captain?"

"Who is this?"

"The name's Blanski."

"Can I help you, Mr. Blanski?" Something in the voice...

"Maybe it's the other way around."

"How's that?"

"There might be something I can do for you."

"Like what?"

"You like the work in Homicide?"

"It keeps me busy, which is why I don't have time to sit and chat. If you've got something to report—"

"It's quite a change from harbor duty, I imagine."

"I beg your pardon?"

"You worked the harbor when I saw you last."

"We've met?"

A sniper. The Harbor detail. *Click.*

"Aw, shit."

"How are you, Barney?"

"I've been better, guy."

He recognized the voice now, as if it were yesterday instead of years ago. Too many years, damn right. The jumbled images of carnage flooded Gibson's mind, his own involvement in the storm that had helped to sweep away some of the city's filth.

And then what? New filth replaced the old.

"I understand you've got a problem with the street gangs," the cool, familiar voice said.

"I'm thinking I've got another problem now."

"Sometimes one problem solves another."

"Or they double up and break my chops."

"It doesn't have to be that way."

The captain cleared his throat. "It might not be the best idea to have this talk right now."

"You short of time?"

"It's more a question of security."

"You want a face-to-face?"

"I want a quiet weekend, but I guess it isn't in the cards."

"Your place or mine?"

"Try neutral ground."

"Sounds fair."

"You know the cross at Golden Gate?"

"Yeah."

"Say, an hour. In the meantime, watch your back."

"It's what I do."

He cradled the receiver, startled to discover that the burning in his gut had faded to a kind of warmth that he could live with. Gibson's pulse was racing faster than his mind, imagining what it could mean.

The Executioner was in town, and maybe Gibson was in for a not-so-instant replay of a nightmare that had also been the captain's finest hour, if looked at in another way.

So many questions.

How had Bolan known he was working Homicide these days? Was it a gamble, reaching out for him at all? A lot of cops bailed out when they did their twenty years, and Gibson would have been long gone if he had joined their ranks.

The wild-assed warrior didn't guess; he knew.

That meant a source inside, or close enough for him to monitor the captain's movements with sufficient certainty to know that Gibson was assigned to work the gang-related kills.

Mack Bolan, shit.

There was a time you couldn't pick the papers up without some mention of his name, and here he was again. A different kind of war, perhaps, but Gibson had no doubt Bolan would be playing by the same old rules. No quarter asked or given to the enemy.

He wondered which was worse—the gangs, or Bolan's way of cleaning out a viper's nest. There were no permanent solutions either way, but it couldn't be denied that the man had a sense of style.

It was an easy two miles from the Hall of Justice to the park. He thought of sounding the alarm, and just as quickly pushed the thought away. How many members of the force remembered Bolan? Would he be taken seriously if he blew the whistle, or would someone think it was time for him to take a hike before the memories intruded too much on reality?

Above all else, he didn't make the call because he still felt grudging admiration for the Executioner, a guy who started out with all the odds against him, turning them around to make it work. In spades.

It took a combination—balls and brains—that was a rare commodity these days. Appeasement was the general rule of thumb in law enforcement as in politics, and all the gas about a "war on drugs" wouldn't change the reality of what went on in court—plea bargains, wrist-slap sentences and prisons with revolving doors.

The same old shit.

Some towns in California had a smaller population than the state's death row, but the condemned had more to fear from old age than from the gas chamber. On the streets it seemed to go from bad to worse each year, without a single bright spot to focus on.

He felt an urge to change all that and recognized the fantasy for what it was. A lone cop wouldn't stand a snowball's chance in hell of making any difference.

It couldn't hurt to have a word with Bolan, even so. The one thing he was sure of was that talk was cheap.

Unless it cost your life.

THE MEET WITH Barney Gibson was a gamble, but the Executioner was trusting instinct when he made the date. His face was different than the one he'd worn the last time they'd met, and he would have ample opportunity to scan the park for stakeouts, going in. Above all else he trusted Gibson as a man who kept his word. A rare breed lately, but they weren't totally extinct.

He had no expectations for the meeting, nothing in the way of an alliance to defeat the local gangs. The captain had a job to do, as always, but their past association offered him an opening in which they could at least negotiate a truce.

No matter how it played, the warrior's San Francisco gig wouldn't last long. Another day or two, if that, and he was on his way. Long-running field campaigns were self-defeating in the context of a warrior working on the outside of the law.

He thought about the team of Stony Man—Hal Brognola, Barbara Price, Aaron Kurtzman and the rest. In spite of his association with the team, he occupied a world apart, divorced from their immediate connection to the federal government. Their operations were sub rosa, but the Executioner's went further, crossing over boundary lines to trespass in the realm of major felonies.

Barney Gibson was a lawman, and he could be damaged by his association with Bolan.

With any luck he might persuade the captain not to interfere beyond the bare requirements of his job. It was a lot to ask, but Bolan understood the way Gibson looked at life, his job, the other side. He recognized the veteran officer's frustration with a system that commanded him to act, then bound his hands and dropped him in the middle of a dogfight, barely able to defend himself.

If he could talk to Gibson, one-on-one, there was a chance they could still work something out before the San Francisco game went into overtime.

A chance, but nothing more.

He put the rental car in motion, driving north through early-evening traffic, one eye on the rearview mirror just in case.

A gamble, right.

But he had always been a gambling man.

7

"Be ready now."

The order was unnecessary, but it made Juice feel more like what he was—a leader for the moment in a war against the family's enemies. A leader had to tell his people what to do from time to time so that they remembered who was running things.

For Juice—born Marvin Green—the Skulls were all the family he had ever really known. His mother was a junkie, and his father had hit the bricks around the time he'd found out she was carrying their second child. A brother, two years older, had been killed by the police at age thirteen, escaping from a holdup in a stolen car. When Marvin started hanging out and living on the streets, his mother had seemed relieved. It gave her more time for the things that mattered. Like her habit.

The Skulls had given the kid somewhere to belong, and he was grateful. More, they'd provided him with something he could fight for when the gang was challenged by competitors or outside enemies.

Like now.

A veteran of the drive-by wars, Juice had two homicides and half a dozen woundings underneath his belt by age sixteen. He also had a birthday coming up, but aging was a process no one in the family took for granted. Ghetto gangsters in their early twenties were considered "old" and Juice couldn't remember any who had reached the big three-oh.

No problem.

Life was meant for living day by day, each hour lifted out of time and savored by itself.

Tonight, for instance.

They were evening a score against the Savage Nomads, and it was a point of pride that One Shot had selected Juice to lead the team. Their target was supposed to be a piece of shit named Jako, a heavy hitter for the Nomads, plus whichever members of the rival gang were hanging out with the guy when he took the fall.

The good news was that Jako had his favorite spots to hang, and he would rarely deviate. A club on Innes Avenue was number one, and if they missed him there, a video arcade on Donahue was next. If all else failed, Juice had his girlfriend's address. They could sail on by and cap the bitch, or maybe catch their target with his pants down.

At the moment they were parked outside of Soul, the club where Jako passed the time at least three nights a week. No special schedule, but he was a regular, and that was all Juice had to know.

His team had drawn an AK-47 and a 12-gauge shotgun from the arsenal. One shooter rode in the front, Juice driving, with the other stuck in back.

"We been here fifteen minutes, man." The beef came from Hammer, who was sitting in the back. "If he was going to show, he would've been here."

"Cool it," Juice commanded. "We got time."

"I don't like sittin' here with all this iron."

"Nobody said you got to like it, cuz. Just *do* it."

"Pigs come by, they are going to gaffle us for spittin' on the sidewalk, cuz."

"Forget about the pigs and keep an eye out for the man."

A sullen silence filled the car. Juice knew his soldiers were on edge, and they had every right to be. Today the Nomads had declared a different kind of war, with no holds barred, and there was no way of predicting who'd be around to talk about it when the smoke cleared. Juice had faith in One Shot and his brother Skulls, but none of them were bulletproof, himself included.

Screw it. If he bought the farm tonight, at least he'd have lived his own life for a little while before it all went down in flames.

"Well, now."

They all knew Jako at a glance, and there was no mistaking his distinctive strut, leading with his gut, broad shoulders rolling in a cocky imitation of the cartoon sailor's stride. He had his arm around some skinny woman, a couple of the other Nomads coming up behind him, sticking close.

So much the better.

Close meant they'd hardly have to aim at all.

Juice twisted the ignition key and felt the engine come alive. There was a problem with the traffic, but he didn't give a damn. The niceties of driver's ed were a low priority when you were wheeling on a drive-by for the Skulls.

He crossed two lanes, leaving protesting horns behind him. He gave them the finger and a big grin in the rearview mirror. It didn't count for shit if someone memorized the plates, since they'd ditch the car within ten minutes, anyway.

The target spotted them and shouted a warning to the others. But there was nowhere they could run to, in the circumstances, because they'd run out of time.

The guns were loud, but Juice held the wheel dead-steady while Cochise and Hammer raked the sidewalk, blasting anything and everything that moved. Juice had a glimpse of Jako going down, his denim jacket rippling with the impacts of high-powered rounds. The other Nomads clawed beneath their clothes for pop guns, as if they had a chance to save themselves.

No fucking way.

Juice took them out of there when it was over, weaving through congested traffic to the proper lane and off the avenue at Donahue. They ditched the hot car at a movie theater where another was waiting in the lot. If anybody saw the transfer, they wouldn't remember details, since the shooters weren't flying colors.

Home free.

They wouldn't really know how well they did until the TV gave a body count, but Juice could feel it in his bones. Clean fucking sweep, or else the next thing to it. A beginning on their payback to the Nomads for the outrage on Arleta Avenue.

But only a beginning.

The war wasn't over yet, by any means.

"I WISH THIS WAS a drive-by," Uzi muttered, fiddling with the safety on his favorite weapon. "Goin' in the fuckin' place, our ass is hangin' out a mile."

"Forget it," Boner said, speaking as the leader of the crew. "We've got to go inside, make sure we don't miss anybody, dig? It's what the Playboy wants."

"The Playboy isn't here."

"You want to tell that to his face sometime?"

"I'll think about it if I don't get snuffed in there."

Their target was an all-soul disco called the Passion Pit, where members of the Skulls were known to congregate. The turnout could be slim tonight, with full-scale warefare shaping up, but Playboy Raymond had decided there were bound to be some Scumbags on the premises. Besides, the very act of tearing up their favorite club would be a measure of retaliation for the strike against the Nomads' clubhouse earlier that day.

It wouldn't even up the books, by any means, but they were getting there.

"All set?"

His shooters gave it back with varying degrees of zeal, but all three answered up. Aside from Uzi, there were Jewels and Popcorn, cuddling their iron and waiting for the words to make a move.

"All right, let's do it."

Covering the compact weapons with their Army surplus jackets, they crossed the street, with Radar waiting in the van to drive them out of there when they were finished raising hell. It shouldn't take too long, considering the crowd and cyclic rate of fire on the selected items they were packing. Boner figured the some civilians were bound to stop a bullet by mistake, but what the hell.

Their colors were at home, and the suspicious bouncer had no call for stopping them, assuming he was man enough to try. It would have bought him pain and death, in any case, so he was wise to stand aside. They had to stand in line and spent three minutes waiting for a chance to step inside.

The club was all smoke and strobe lights, when they made it, dancers spinning on the floor and cracking splits as if they thought they were M.C. Hammer, or maybe Michael Jackson. Rap sounds throbbed from the speakers mounted every thirty feet or so around the walls, so it was pretty much a waste of time to talk.

No biggee. Boner had been practicing his hand signs, getting ready for a job like this, and his selected shooters understood the silent rap. Two drifted off in the direction of the bar, while Boner teamed with Uzi, fading to the right. They were supposed to start the party on his signal, once they spotted any Skulls on the premises and got a decent fix.

Okay.

In front of him at two o'clock three members of the Skulls were sitting at a table with their women, nursing beer.

They were on target, close enough to score without half aiming in the murky atmosphere. Across the room, if Boner squinted, it appeared that Jewels and Popcorn had another group of Skulls in their sights.

"All right."

Boner pulled back his Army surplus jacket as his finger found the trigger of his KG-99. The music nearly covered it at first, his chosen target jerking like a dancer trying out new moves, except that he was dancing in his chair and spilling beer across the table as he fell.

The others joined in. The music stuttered, died, and Boner couldn't tell if one of them had hit the jukebox, or if someone had simply yanked the plug. Whatever, he was letting rip and watching bodies topple, getting off on the explosive sound and muzzle-flashes, breathing in the gunsmoke, easily absorbing the concussive recoil of his weapon.

This was how it ought to be around the clock, he thought. The Savage Nomads kicking ass and taking names.

That kind of gig was over when your prey started shooting back or you ran out of bullets. The way it happened, both things went down almost simultaneously, shots from one of the surviving Scumbags knocking Popcorn on his ass about the same time that the magazine on Boner's KG-99 clicked dry.

"Shag ass!" he barked at Uzi, heading for the door and trying to reload as frightened people jostled him on every side. Another burst ripped behind him, and he only hoped his backup understood that they were pulling out.

There was no sign of Popcorn as they hit the exit running, Jewels a step ahead of Boner on the run back to their waiting van. He didn't know how many people they'd wasted back there, but he figured half a dozen, anyway. Not bad for taking potluck on an evening when the Scumbags should have been alert and taking care of business in a new gang war.

A war they had started in the first place.

Stupid bastards, taking five while every Savage Nomad in the city was out looking for their asses. It served them right to die like pigs without a fighting chance.

He thought of Popcorn, wondering if he was dead, but there was no way they could hang around and check it out. The guy was either breathing or he wasn't. If he was, then Popcorn knew enough to keep his mouth shut when the pigs came calling. Give them nothing they couldn't pick up from the daily news.

The van was rolling, free and clear. Behind them in the rearview, Boner made out milling figures on the sidewalk, a couple of them flying colors for the Skulls. It was tempting to go back and finish them, but he'd done enough for one night.

Make your score and back off while you've got the chance. Don't ever press your luck.

A lesson learned.

And it was party time.

EARL WEATHERS SAT and listened to the radio reports, disgusted with himself that there was nothing he could do. Gang Intervention was a joke on nights like this when everything just simply came unglued and fell apart.

It was a goddamn madhouse on the streets tonight, and he was sidelined on a desk recording incidents and keeping track of the events as they went down. Some kind of marvelous example to his officer and to the youngsters they supposedly were working overtime to rescue from the life-and-death dominion of the gangs.

No, "rescue" wouldn't fit. He had no starry-eyed illusions of himself eradicating urban crime and saving fractured families. The best he could hope for, Weathers knew, was just to make a difference when and where he could—prevent a drive-by shooting now and then, or urge some frightened individual to think again before he joined a gang and started pushing crack.

Most times he failed. And when the failure left a body on the sidewalk, Weathers grudgingly made room for Homicide. It undercut Gang Intervention's power, giving up the biggest cases when they had a chance to put some thug away, but that was politics in the department, and he understood the rules.

Right now he needed to talk to Captain Barney Gibson, to help coordinate their actions on the hits that had been going down since dusk. The feud between the Skulls and Savage Nomads was exploding into open warefare, bodies scattered everywhere, with no end in sight.

If GIU meant anything—if it was going to survive the week—they had to be involved in sorting out the current wrangle on the streets. There simply was no other way to make it work.

And yet he hated eating crow, the kind of feeling he got from going to another PD branch with hat in hand and asking if they wouldn't mind his sitting in. A job like this should have fallen on his desk by rights.

There was a flip side, though. If things went sour—and it looked that way increasingly from where Earl Weathers sat—the major heat would fall on Homicide for failure to prevent or clear the cases that were piling up from Hunters Point to the Embarcadero. Barney Gibson might not be the kind of guy Weathers would take home to meet his family, but he was still a cop, and it was rough to see that kind of shit come down on anyone.

Okay. Pick up the goddamn telephone and make the call.

He did.

A gruff voice came on the line for Homicide, informing him that Captain Gibson had been called away. The stand-in couldn't say when Gibson would be back, and he had no idea where the captain was.

"If you want to call back in the morning, he should be here sometime after—"

"How about we page him?" Weathers answered, biting off an expletive before it passed his lips.

"Jeez, I don't know."

"Your call, I guess. Of course, it has to do with all these gang-related shootings he's been working on. I guess he won't mind waiting overnight to get the news. Your name again?"

"I don't think paging him's a problem," the detective from Homicide said, not quite so gruffly. "Can't promise he'll call in, understand. Some guys, they take the beepers off and leave them home."

"I'll take a chance."

"Okay. And who's the callback for?"

"Lieutenant Weathers, GIU."

"I got it down. If the captain calls back in, he'll get the word."

"Terrific."

Hanging up, Earl Weathers felt as if he were caught up in some kind of tacky vaudeville show. Perhaps a situation comedy, where the participants run in and out of different rooms, just missing one another every time.

He'd give the captain thirty minutes on the dot before he started pulling strings himself. No way did he intend to sit out this gang war behind a desk and watch his own career become one of the casualties.

If Gibson couldn't help him, Weathers was prepared to help himself.

8

The giant Prayer Book Cross in Golden Gate Park was famous with Clint Eastwood fans as the site where "Dirty Harry" Callahan confronted the deadly Scorpio and both men nearly lost their lives. In real life there had never been a shoot-out beneath the looming cross, and Bolan hoped to leave the city with that record still intact.

It was a given, going in, that he wouldn't resist with deadly force if the police turned out en masse. He had a few tricks up his sleeve for such occasions, but he wouldn't draw down on a cop. Case closed.

The good news was that Bolan trusted Barney Gibson—to a point at least. The captain had sworn an oath, but a simple meet with the Executioner wouldn't demand that he call out the cavalry. They'd already been around the block together in years gone by, and Gibson had decided it was possible to coexist with Bolan under given circumstances.

Even so, times change, and people with them. The warrior wouldn't take anything for granted.

Cross Over Drive bisected the park a hundred yards due west of Stow Lake and Strawberry Hill, winding north to south. As soon as Bolan had the chance, he made a right-hand turn on John F. Kennedy Drive. He passed below the cross and kept on driving slowly through a scattering of joggers, strollers and lovers holding hands until he reached the parking lot for the De Young Museum. The place was closed, of course, but visitors still used the parking lot while they struck off to make a jogging circuit of the lake or tour the Japanese tea garden nearby. Mild weather helped the turnout, and he parked beside a family station wagon, watching out for any "unmarked" cars that would betray a stakeout in the area.

No rush. He still had plenty of time, and the cross was nearly visible from where he stood a thousand yards away. A bank of floodlights marked the spot at night, a beacon to the faithful or the hopeless, holding out an invitation thousands took advantage of each month. Some came to pray, or merely have their picture snapped beside the biggest crucifix they would ever see. The graffiti artists stayed away, and that, the Executioner reflected, was a miracle of sorts.

He took his time returning to the cross, not following the road exactly, veering off to see if anyone would follow on foot. No takers, but he couldn't rule out spotters stationed at a distance, tracking his with scopes or even shotgun mikes to monitor his words.

It finally came down to trust, and he'd have to play the situation as it came.

At least, he thought, there was no sign of Skulls or Savage Nomads in the park. The scattered passersby were mixed, their numbers far from lily-white, but teenage gangsters would have been a standout, even so. His distance from the pavement let him spot approaching cars and take a hasty reading on their occupants.

All clear so far.

In deference to his mission the Executioner was traveling light. He wore the sleek Beretta 93-R in a shoulder sling designed to take the custom silencer, as well, and spare magazines beneath his right arm in a double pouch. He'd considered carrying a smoke grenade or two in case he had to ditch a foot pursuit, but Bolan wound up taking Barney Gibson at his word.

It was a luxury, this thing called trust, but Gibson hadn't let him down before.

First time for everything, a small voice in his brain reminded, but Bolan cut it off. If there was no one he could trust outside of Stony Man Farm, then he'd waged his one-man war in vain.

From a hundred yards away he saw two couples standing by the cross, illuminated by the floods. He waited, willing them to leave, but he resisted glancing at his watch, a futile show of nerves. Gibson might not mind having company, provided no one had a chance to overhear their words.

Five minutes.

Bolan started forward, moving at an easy pace to close the final distance. Gibson knew the risk of interruption when he chose a public meeting place, and the warrior would present himself on time. It would be Gibson's call from there, and if he didn't show, so be it.

The foursome moved away at his approach, not glancing at him really, acting on the city dweller's instinct to avoid a stranger in the dark.

The warrior lingered on the fringes of the light, aware that it was time. He heard a sound behind him. Someone was drawing closer and made no attempt to hide.

A familiar voice asked, "Are you a praying man?"

SECURITY WAS UPPERMOST on Barney Gibson's mind throughout the crosstown drive to keep his date with Bolan in the park. He checked his rearview mirror constantly and kept an ear cocked toward the two-way radio for any messages that might suggest a setup or a tail.

He told himself he was getting paranoid, but it did little good. He'd been playing office politics around the Hall of Justice long enough to know the walls had ears, and while his telephone might not be monitored, he wouldn't put it past the brass to keep an eye on their subordinates—especially in a situation like the present one, where Gibson was assigned to an explosive case with no real leads or hope of a solution in the next few hours.

Gibson knew the chief would shit a brick if he knew a captain out of Homicide was meeting with the man some still remembered as the Executioner, no matter what the rationale. That kind of news could sink administrations if it leaked, and politicians—in or out of uniform—were always after ways to shift the blame before the roof fell in.

He parked his unmarked cruiser and locked it before walking back toward the cross. A solitary figure stood on the fringe of light, more silhouette than substance.

It stood to reason that he wouldn't recognize the Executioner's face. Mack Bolan hadn't lived this long without acquiring certain attributes of the chameleon. When the "war" began, his enemies had known the face he'd been born with, so he changed it. The face was new before he ever came to San Francisco and charged into Barney Gibson's life. With his reported death in New York City some years later, it made sense that Bolan would have changed again.

But you could almost *feel* the guy, for God's sake, even if you didn't know him. He possessed a kind of aura that was more than violence, way beyond the simple smell of death some killers carried with them like a whiff of tawdry after-shave.

It was more like a kind of power, if you had to spell it out . . . and even that wasn't exactly right. A strength, without the bully's need to prove himself by pushing other folks around. The Executioner had proved himself so often that there was nothing left to prove, but he kept butting heads against the odds.

Coming up on Bolan's flank, not trying for his blind side, Gibson closed the range to thirty feet before he spoke.

"Are you a praying man?"

The warrior turned his new face to a friend and said, "Not lately. Maybe I should start."

"I guess you do okay without."

"How's Homicide?"

"I've got them lined up, dying for attention," Gibson said. "Why don't we take a walk?"

"Suits me."

They started on a circuit of the lake, and Gibson got directly to the business that was on his mind. "You're taking on the gangs."

"I'm looking into it."

"From what I've seen today you're looking pretty hard."

"It's overdue."

"Why not L.A.?" the captain asked. "They've got some guys down there that make our assholes look like choirboys."

"Maybe later," Bolan replied. "This is where I am right now."

"It's not the safest place to be," Gibson said. "What I hear around the shop, the gangs are catching federal heat. You might be getting more flack than you bargained for unless..."

The warrior paused and faced him. "What?"

"Forget it."

There was no point digging up the rumors of a federal link with Bolan, speculation that he might be running covert operations for a branch of government so secret that it didn't even have a name. That kind of talk was always rife in cases where the fugitive had lots of ink. Some folks still thought John Dillinger had set up a patsy at the Biograph and made his getaway to Mexico. Conspiracies were seen behind the deaths of popes and presidents and aging rock stars, most of them so far beyond the realm of plausibility they sounded more like science fiction than the "inside scoop."

They kept on walking and spotted flashlights bobbing on the slope of Strawberry Hill in the middle of the lake.

"I don't suppose you have a fix on when you're leaving town."

"Not yet. Another day or so with any luck."

"Why is it that a day with you reminds me of the year I spent with Doug MacArthur in Korea?"

Bolan frowned. "The war was here before I came to town," he pointed out. "From what I understand, it's been here for at least two years."

"Hell, I know that. I'm working Homicide, remember? I get sick to death of seeing kids zipped up in rubber bags. I just don't want to see this city torn apart."

"That isn't in the plan."

"You're not the only one with plans, you know."

"Right now the Skulls and Nomads have an ax to grind with each other. If I help them out, we might clip two heads for the price of one."

"And in the meantime who gets wasted in the cross fire?"

"Who got wasted in the cross fire yesterday?" Bolan asked. "What about the day before? Last week? I didn't have a chance to make a list before I took the job."

"Okay. My point is, these punks aren't the old-line Mob. With the Sicilians there was always a pretense of honor, basic rules they play by in their own self-interest to avoid some heat. The street gangs have no concept of restraint. They'll strafe a whole damn neighborhood because some member of the opposition lives there. They don't even have to see him on the street."

"More reason why they should be stopped."

"So what's the plan?"

"I'm not enlisting allies," Bolan said.

"Who's volunteering? I'd just like to have a hint about who's doing what before the shit comes down for real."

"I'm looking at divide and conquer as the way to go. The Skulls and Nomads hate each other as it is. A little push and I should have all the extra guns I need."

"Together with a shitload of civilian casualties," the captain stated.

"If you want to help, keep pressure on the gangs. Surveillance doesn't cramp my style that much."

"I've noticed. Look, the heat from this is bound to have them hopping mad at city hall."

"I hope so. If the power structure had been hopping mad before, the Skulls and Nomads wouldn't own the streets in Hunters Point."

"We walk a razor's edge these days," Gibson said. "Charge a black with any crime, no matter what the evidence, and we've got half a dozen groups proclaiming 'racist genocide' before we get the little darling booked. That's something else you might consider, presswise, while you've still got time to walk."

"I never read my own reviews," the Executioner replied. "You know as well as I do this is no more race or civil rights than crack cocaine is modern medicine. The animals I'm looking at would still be savages if they were white, red, green or blue."

"*I* know that," Gibson told him, "but we're still in liberal San Francisco, if you get my drift. We're not that far away from riots in the Point, Black Panthers, Zebra murders... Jesus, I just hope you watch your step."

"I always do."

"And my name's Howard Hughes. If you want me to, I'll put you in my will along with Melvin Dumar and the Bobbsey twins."

"Sounds good to me."

"You're on." He felt the crooked smile begin to slip and couldn't hold it even when he tried. "So tell me, how can I help out?"

"I told you—"

"I know what you told me. If you think I'm sitting on my hands while you go one-on-one against both gangs, you must be ready for a Section 8."

"Too risky."

"What the hell? I could have bailed out years ago. If they want to cut me loose, I've got more pension coming than most guys who pull the pin at twenty."

"You can't spend it in the joint."

"Forget it, copper, they'll never take me alive."

"Goddamn it, Barney."

"Hey, you should have thought about this shit before you made your move."

"I did," Bolan said. "I was thinking wisdom came with age."

"Strike three. Call this my midlife crisis if you want. I'm in."

"The only thing I really need is space, some combat stretch. It's better if I don't run into SWAT teams every time I turn around."

"I'll see what I can do. Of course, you understand I'm not in charge of Homicide, much less Gang Intervention or the special teams we roll on hotshot calls."

"That's understood."

"I might be able to confuse the issue, buy a little time, but if they start to ask me what the hell's going on—"

"Then you look out for number one. I wouldn't have it any other way."

"How long since you looked out for number one?"

"I do it every day."

"I'm sure."

"You think I'd be here if I played it any other way?"

"No sale. I've seen you work, remember? It's one for all, okay, but I don't see much in the way of all for one."

"I do all right," the Executioner replied.

"I don't hear me complaining. I only wondered if it doesn't wear you down sometimes."

Dumb question, right, but it was out before he had a chance to bite his tongue.

"Let's say I'm getting by."

"You might want to consider R and R when you get this thing behind you."

"Yeah, I might at that."

Fat chance, the captain thought, but he had made the effort.

"I wouldn't want to see you walk the plank on this one," Gibson said after a pair of pretty joggers retreated from earshot.

"I can promise you it isn't what I had in mind."

"Plans change with circumstance," the captain answered. "You know that as well as I do."

"I'm on top of it right now. I never second-guess tomorrow."

The pager on his belt distracted Gibson, and he cursed beneath his breath before he turned it off. "More action, I suppose."

"I wouldn't be surprised."

"One thing. What happens when you're finished with the Skulls and Nomads, if you get that far? The boys at GIU have charts on three, four dozen other gangs in town. It won't take long to fill that vacuum at the top."

"I never claimed to have a cure-all," Bolan answered honestly. "The new gangs coming up, at least you have your handle going in. There must be something you can use against them in the growing stage before they get too big and strong."

"I hope so."

"So do I."

"If not, I guess that makes the rest of it a waste of time."

The soldier frowned and shook his head. "Not even close. The savages I stop today are stopped forever. No more rapes and murders, break-ins, robberies or drive-bys, drug deals in the schoolyard. If someone moves in afterward to take their place, you start from scratch and learn from past mistakes, nail down the cases one step at a time."

"You make it sound so easy."

"Wrong. You've got the hard part, playing by the book. I get short-term results in record time because I've thrown the book away. You never had that luxury."

"I don't think I could handle it to tell the truth."

"No reason why you should. Society's in trouble if the book gets thrown away for good."

"Selective editing?"

"When things get too far out of hand, somebody has to jerk the leash. It doesn't mean we need Gestapo tactics all the time."

"I don't know why I'm arguing. You've got me sold. Let's say I want to hear how some of this will sound at my review board when they can my ass."

"It won't come down to that."

"You hope."

"Whatever happens, no one hears your name from me. That's guaranteed."

Gibson knew he could take it to the bank without a solitary reservation in his mind. The rest boiled down to self-control, and whether he could play a sideline waiting game while Bolan took the heat and gave it back in spades.

"You'll keep in touch then?" Gibson asked.

"Absolutely."

"What's that handle I remember—"

"Striker."

"There you go. I'll be on standby for his call. Right now I've got a few calls of my own to make."

"Take care."

"You, too. I mean that."

Bolan smiled and turned away without another word, the shadows taking him as Barney Gibson cursed himself and started searching for a public telephone.

9

Corey Souders was already waiting in her father's living room when he came home. He was surprised to see her, and concern was written on his face.

"I thought you had a class."

"I'm cutting, Father." He wouldn't be "Daddy" while they had this little talk.

"Are you all right? Is something wrong?"

"That seems to be the question I should ask."

"I don't know what you mean."

"I followed you this evening when you left the park. In Portia's car, the blue Chevette. Remember I told you mine was running rough."

"I'm curious to know why you'd do a thing like that," he said at last.

"Because I knew you lied to the police. I don't mind that so much, but then you also lied to me."

"You think so?"

"Father, I'm not blind, and you should know by now that you didn't raise a stupid child."

"That's true. Sometimes I think you might be too smart for your own self-interest."

Corey smiled at that. "I wouldn't be the only one."

"You followed me, you said."

"That's right. I saw your friend."

"Associate."

"Who is he, Father?"

"I see nothing to be gained by telling you his name."

"Or sharing it with the police?"

"He's a federal officer from Washington. The nature of his work is confidential. The police might interfere or actively obstruct him if they knew he was working in the city."

"So? Since when is that our problem?"

"Since *I* asked the man to come here."

"About the gangs?"

"I really don't appreciate your cutting class to play detective, Corey."

"Oh, but I'm supposed to sit back and applaud while you play Junior G-man, putting everything you have at risk."

"I've been at risk, if you recall, since I first spoke out publicly against the gangs in Hunters Point. That hasn't changed, nor will it if I simply sit around and wait for the police to count their paper clips."

"Who *is* this federal man? What does he do exactly?"

"He investigates potential danger situations and attempts to find solutions with the means at hand."

"He's from the FBI, or what?"

"I will not be interrogated, Corey, least of all by you."

The words were like a slap across her face. She saw regret in her father's eyes, but he couldn't recant without inviting other questions in the wake of his retreat.

"Well, since you're playing secret agent, Father, you won't mind if I do likewise. It should make good practice for investigating cases when I get to law school."

"Corey, I forbid—"

"I beg your pardon?" Sudden anger heated her cheeks. *"You forbid?"*

"You just don't understand the danger—"

"Don't I, Father? This is *my* home, where they've tried to kill *my* father once before. If that's not good enough, I watch the news. I think I understand the danger perfectly."

"You should be concentrating on your education," he informed her, "getting out of here to build a better life."

"Suppose I decide to use my education here among the people I grew up with. Who can help them better than a native from the Point? I always thought that's why you stayed to face the gangs when Mama died."

"And I regret it every godforsaken day."

"But you keep fighting."

"It's the only way I know to live my life."

"That's why I love you, Daddy. And it's also why I won't be bullied into quitting, just because there's risk involved."

He frowned again. "It wasn't just the gangs I had in mind. If you start messing with police or butting into federal business, you could find yourself in jail before you know it. Charges of obstructing justice won't impress the law school screening board."

"I'll take my chances." Corey was uncertain whether she was hanging tough from her convictions, or because she found it virtually impossible to knuckle under where her father was concerned.

"Well, I suppose you'll have to do what you think best," he said resignedly, and for an instant Corey thought his mind was drifting elsewhere, something she'd witnessed only at her father's times of greatest stress.

"Are you okay, Dad?"

"Hmm? Oh, yes, I'm fine. Just wondering where I'll get money for your bail when San Francisco's finest lock you up for stepping on their toes."

"I'm not that clumsy. They won't even know I'm there."

"My daughter, Shirley Holmes."

"Believe it, when I need to be."

She'd been hoping for a smile—or, better yet, a full confession of the secret he was clearly hiding—but she had to settle for a sad expression, almost one of loss.

"What is it, Dad?"

"There are people dying on the street tonight for no good reason, Corey. I don't want you being part of that."

"Relax. You know I'm not a wild-eyed militant."

"As if that made a difference. Mrs. Jackson wasn't marching off to war the afternoon they shot her by mistake outside Safeway. Tommy Porter died because his paper route ran past a crack house, and he passed along that way when there was trouble in the neighborhood. You know the names as well as I do, girl."

"That's right. And I believe we owe them something."

"So do I. But I can't function with the only living member of my family breathing down my neck and always standing in the line of fire."

A glint of tears shone in the man's eyes, the first that she'd seen since they'd come home from her mother's funeral.

"Daddy, hey, I didn't know it meant this much."

"Well, now you do."

"Okay, I promise," she said, squirming inwardly with discomfort at the bald-faced lie. "All better now?"

"I'm getting there."

"If I hurry, maybe I can make the last part of that class."

"That's my girl."

SOUDERS GAVE HER POINTS for trying, but Corey couldn't pull the wool over his eyes that easily. He saw through his daughter as if her flesh and bones were made of glass, and most of what he saw on those irregular inspections made him swell his chest with pride. There was the stubbornness, of course; she got that trait from him more than her mother, but it wasn't any major thing.

Unless sometime it got her killed.

If Souders knew his daughter—and he did—she'd continue with her quest for information on his secret contact until she unearthed the information she was looking for . . . or someone stopped her cold.

It was the latter possibility that worried Souders most.

He knew Corey was a bright young woman, near the top of every class she took, but book-smart was a different thing from street-smart. Growing up in Hunters Point, per se, didn't ensure that every child was educated in the fine points of survival at the lower levels of society. If they had loving parents who provided for their needs, as Corey Souders had, they often missed the street scene, or observed it from a distance with a faint taste of disdain.

It was a good thing she'd missed all that, Souders thought, but the shortage in her street-smarts might be deadly now. If she went poking into things that should be better left alone, inevitably Corey would encounter someone ready to defend his secrets at the risk of human life.

Her life.

He wished he could get in touch with Blanski, but the man from Washington had left no contact number. He was on the move, unreachable until such time as he checked in with Souders for the latest news.

And what would Souders tell him when he called? That Corey was resigned to play detective, and that Blanski ought to guard against the danger of an unarmed college girl screwing up his plans?

Those plans themselves made Souders nervous. He had made the call to Washington in desperation, seeking help that the police couldn't—or wouldn't—offer at the local level. In his heart he'd expected something in the nature of a brush-off, possibly a phone call from the FBI or Justice to remind him they had no jurisdiction in a local case.

Instead, he was confronted with a stranger whose credentials were suspect at best, and whose methods were as violent—if not more so—than the gangs'. He'd been willing to dismiss the massacre at Bay Front Park as self-defense, a case of do or die, but it was obvious from recent news that Blanski had been turning up the heat with further strikes against the Skulls and Nomads, nudging them toward total war.

The worst of it was feeling left out of the action, thinking back to Vietnam and younger days when he had stalked the jungle trails in search of Victor Charlie. It was a shock for Souders to admit he missed the hunt, and he was forced to look inside himself, to see what kind of man he had become.

The worst part about remembering that morning in the park was the realization that he'd been less shocked than he expected. Part of him was cheering when the punks went down, a little taste of payback for the misery they'd inflicted on his neighbors during the past two years. It did him good to see those little bastards stuck on the receiving end, their cocky smiles erased once and for all.

There was no way he could team up with Blanski for the action yet to come. He had to think about the here and now, and that meant Corey, too.

She was beyond his reach, and there was nothing he could do to drag her back again.

He settled in to watch and wait. Perhaps to pray, if he hadn't forgotten how.

THE WAREHOUSE NORTH of Lockwood was used by members of the Savage Nomads as a dump for military weapons stolen from the naval yard at Hunters Point. Within the past eight months, since they'd bribed two members of the Shore Patrol, the gang had managed to abscond with M-16s, Beretta semiautomatic pistols and a few grenades. When there was heat, they laid off for a while and waited for the Navy to relax its guard again.

No sweat.

The warehouse was on Bolan's list of targets, passed along by Vernon Souders, though he wasn't certain of its contents as he made his drive-by in the dark. The warrior saw a vintage Lincoln Continental and a low-slung Datsun pickup parked against the loading dock, no guards in sight as Bolan drove on past and parked a half block farther west.

He used the shadows on the return trip, his blacksuit helping him to blend with the shadows. He wore the 93-R in its shoulder rig, the Desert Eagle semiauto .44 in military leather on his hip. The satchel charge he carried was especially prepared for what he had in mind.

It was the standard warehouse layout, with a metal ladder bolted to the wall on one side, granting Bolan access to the roof. Four skylights were up there, along with the compressors for an air conditioner the present occupants had never used. The San Francisco weather was a dream in spring and summer; if it got a little chilly in the winter, what the hell? The merchandise was never going to complain.

Topside, he moved with cautious steps across the roof until he reached the nearest skylight, peering down inside the warehouse. It was not as full as it could be, some crates and matériel clustered near the center of the room, with lots of space around the sides. He had to shift to the next skylight before he stood directly over the assembled goods.

Unclipping smoke grenades, he knelt and set them on the metal roof within arm's reach. That done, he opened the canvas satchel, set the timer and closed the flap again. The basic charge was C-4 plastique, with a hot incendiary kicker to ensure the maximum destruction when it blew. He gave himself a minute and a half to clear the roof and hoped it would be enough.

They kept the skylight locked, of course. With the Beretta set for 3-round bursts he pulled the trigger twice and saw the plate-glass box disintegrate, a swarm of razor fragments raining down. He dropped the satchel and watched as it bounced and disappeared between two standing crates.

Voices shouted at him from the warehouse floor below, and he heard a gunshot well before the shooter had a chance to aim. He pitched the smoke grenades, already hissing as they fell, and started for the ladder at a run. Behind him automatic gunfire ripped through the shattered skylight wasted on the stars.

He scrambled down the ladder, already halfway to the bottom when he heard the sound of running feet below. He hung on with one hand, drew the heavy Magnum with the other and swiveled to face the threat.

Two Nomads were below him, both with weapons in their hands. The Desert Eagle bucked and bellowed twice, 240 grains of death exploding through one startled face and blowing it away before the second gunner took his in the chest. He left them twitching on the loading dock and had a fair lead toward his rental when the warehouse went to hell.

The C-4 blast was slightly muffled by the building, but it literally raised the roof... a portion of it, anyway. The metal walls bowed outward, rippling visibly, with doors and windows emptied by the shock wave. He was watching as the thermite charges followed, flinging white-hot coals around the warehouse to devour everything they touched, including steel, concrete, the earth itself. If there was any screaming from the center of the funeral pyre, it never reached his ears.

Another hot potato for the Homicide division, but the hit was swift and clean. A fire alarm was mounted on a phone pole near the spot where he'd parked his vehicle, and the warrior rang it in before he drove away.

The Skulls and Nomads should be at each other's throats by now. He knew the risk to innocent civilians, but he had a plan in mind to isolate the warring gangs and take them down together at a site of Bolan's own selection. First, though, he'd have to stir the pot a little more and bring it to a roiling boil.

The heat was on, and the Executioner was turning up the fire.

10

The fire was nearly out when Barney Gibson got there, rolling on the call, with smoke and flashing colored lights enough to guide him for the last few blocks to the blackened hulk that had once been a warehouse.

Two bodies had been dragged clear of the flames and draped with sheets, awaiting Homicide and someone from the medical examiner's office to clear them for removal to the morgue. An ambulance was standing by, the young attendants watching firemen go about their job and looking vaguely bored.

A uniformed policeman was waiting for him with the bodies.

"What's going down?"

"These two were shot, the way it looks," the sergeant answered. "Hard to figure out exactly with the warehouse trashed that way. My guess would be that they met somebody going in or coming out. The shooter set the charge before he split."

"What charge?"

"I talked to Quimby on the arson squad. He's over there with the battalion chief. He figures thermite, or some other kind of military shit like that. I told him someone would be stopping by."

"Okay."

Reluctantly he knelt beside the shrouded bodies, peeling back each sheet in turn. Both were young blacks, flying Nomad colors when they died. One had an entrance wound off-center to the face beside his nose, some kind of heavy round that mushroomed going in and blew the left rear section of his skull away with most of what had been inside. The other's flannel shirt was sopping red, and Gibson didn't bother looking for the wound above his heart.

"These two are it?" he asked.

The sergeant shrugged. "They haven't had a chance to poke around inside."

"Well, damn."

"Looks like a hot time in the old town tonight."

He dropped the sheets back into place and rose to cross the parking lot between two fire trucks, searching out Joe Quimby from the fire department's arson squad. The pudgy, balding man saw Gibson coming, breaking off his conversation with the battalion commander to meet Gibson halfway.

"You've had a busy night, I understand," he said in greeting.

"Let's just say I could have done without the barbecue."

"Somebody did a job all right. We're looking at a chemical accelerant on top of an explosive charge. I'll be surprised if it's not thermite when the tests come back."

"What kind of an explosive charge?"

"We won't know for a while, but it was heavy-duty, I can tell you that. These kids are playing with the real McCoy."

"I guess."

"One other thing," Quimby said. "There was ammo going off inside when Number Eight arrived. That tells me they were storing arms and ammunition here. We'll have more details for you once this mess cools off enough to sift the wreckage."

Gibson nodded, wondering how many cindered corpses they'd find inside when it was possible to check. Another blowout for the Executioner, with Gibson picking up the pieces, feeling rather like a garbageman.

He shrugged the feeling off. They had a deal, of sorts, and he was holding up his end. When they identified the two dead shooters in the parking lot, he had no doubt their faces would be staring at him from a mug book at the Hall of Justice. On the average, Skulls and Nomads ten or fifteen crimes apiece in any given six-month period.

Small loss. And if there were a few more fried inside the warehouse, it wouldn't make Gibson lose a moment's sleep. For all intents and purposes, as decent human beings, these punks had been dead the day they joined the gang.

The bad news was that Bolan's full-scale war was swiftly taking shape. The call he made from Golden Gate alerted Gibson to a rash of incidents that had continued through the past three hours—drive-by shootings, one pitched battle at a soul club in the Point, some vandalism linked by fresh graffiti to the warring gangs.

Compelled to boast, they sometimes went out of their way to warn intended victims, like a pool shark calling shots before he scored. Walls blossomed with the names of targets and a red 187, lifted from the California Penal Code for murder. On occasion the intended mark was wise enough to split. More often, idiot machismo made him stand his ground or take the battle to his enemies before they tracked him down.

It was all in deadly earnest, from their inbred hatred to the martial hardware they employed.

What kind of freak show was he living in where youths went to war for drugs or killed one another over insults that another generation would have settled with a swift punch in the nose? Were the established gangs a cancer eating at the vitals of society, or were they just a symptom of a deeper, more malignant rot?

Too many questions for a homicide detective on a busy night in San Francisco. He had work to do, reports to write, and it would be a challenge not to mention one Mack Bolan when he started summing up the evening's carnage.

Room to breathe.

That was all the soldier had asked for, and it sounded like a simple thing until you realized that giving Bolan room to breathe meant that someone else *stopped* breathing right away. How many yet to go before the storm was past?

One thing you could bank on with the Executioner—whatever happened, it would happen fast.

The Skulls and Nomads hadn't seen the worst of it, by any means. Which meant that Barney Gibson hadn't, either.

He'd paid the money for his ticket on the roller coaster, and there was nothing he could do from this point on but hold on tight and take his chances with the ride.

THE GUNNER'S NAME was Popeye. He was barely twenty years old, and he'd killed three Savage Nomads in the past eleven months. His reputation as a trigger man was well established in the Skulls, and he was treated with respect.

Accordingly the mission he'd drawn this night was one considered vital to the family. With three Skulls of his own selection he was under orders to decapitate the enemy by wasting Playboy Raymond and the Nomads' general command staff, if he could. As an alternative, the strike force was assigned to kill as many of the opposition as they could within the next few hours, forcing Playboy and his tribe to sue for peace.

A lot of good it would do them, sucking up to One Shot Johnson after they'd treacherously launched the war, but it wasn't in Popeye's job description to dispute his orders. He didn't come equipped to plot strategic miracles, but he could carry out his orders with the best.

At half past nine his team was parked outside a smallish house on Cochrane Street where Playboy and his second-in-command reportedly had taken shelter after the attack on their compound earlier that day. There was no sign of Raymond or his buddies yet, except for two guards on the porch, but that was fine. If no one surfaced in another ten or fifteen minutes, they were going in to waste everybody on the premises.

His troops were ready, armed with automatic rifles, submachine guns and a couple of grenades—one frag and one concussion, and he meant to use them both if they were forced to fight their way inside.

It would be easier, of course, if Playboy should decide to take himself a little drive, come out just long enough for Popeye and his men to aim, squeeze off a couple of dozen well-placed rounds and drive away.

Sweet dreams.

Experience had taught him that the easy way was seldom how things went down in the world. You had to work for what you got within established limits, and it didn't matter whether you were pushing crack or sitting out a contract. Anything worth doing was worth doing right.

"What's that?"

His driver, Low Ball, had a bony index finger aiming down the block, where Popeye saw dark sedan approaching from the north. No lights were on, and the car was creeping up along the curb, suspicious like.

"Ain't ours," Popeye said. "Everybody get your shit together now!"

Downrange, the Nomads sentries had their full attention focused on the car, as well, one of them reaching underneath his jacket for a weapon while the other stepped back toward the door, prepared to warn the house if anything went down.

"It doesn't look like—"

"Hush!"

Confusion made Popeye lose his train of thought if anybody spoke within the car. He concentrated on the dark sedan, palms moist against the cool steel of the Uzi in his lap. They'd have recognized a pigmobile at once, but this was something else. And if their enemies didn't appear to recognize the car...

"Hey!"

A hand came out the driver's window, balancing a stubby weapon that reminded Popeye of a sawed-off shotgun, only fatter. He was watching as the weapon belched a single round, the porch of Playboy Raymond's hideout suddenly erupting in a ball of flame that punched the sentries through an awkward somersault and dumped them in the middle of the yard.

There was a heartbeat of hesitation as the shooter drew his weapon back inside the car, then the head-lights came alive, half blinding Popeye with their sudden brilliance.

"Who the fuck *is* that?" his driver asked.

"Ain't ours," he repeated. "We better waste the motherfucker just in case."

He heard a window cranking down behind him on the left, and someone pulling back an AK-47's cocking bolt. He brought up the Uzi, prepared to squeeze off through the windshield if he had to for a clear shot at his unknown enemy.

The dark sedan surged forward, laying rubber on the road, and Popeye felt his stomach rolling as the stubby weapon slid back into view. This time the muzzle was directed toward the car in which he sat. It seemed grotesquely large, some kind of cannon fitted with a stock and pistol grip.

He panicked, groping for the handle on his door and finding it. The dome light blazed above him, startling his companions, causing one of them to curse. He had a leg out of the car, a foot on the sidewalk, when the stubby weapon flashed. He could *see* the fat projectile coming. Jesus, he could—

The concussion threw him clear and dropped him facedown in the middle of a scruffy yard, his nostrils filled with smoke, a burning stench that emanated from the car, himself, the very air he tried to breathe. Popeye had no feeling in his legs, and he was glad of that, because he feared they were broken, maybe even gone.

There was a secondary blast, the gas tank going, and he heard the grass around him start to crackle as it caught from burning gasoline. It was an effort, and it brought his screaming legs to life, and Popeye knew he had to move his ass or get it toasted where he lay.

With grim determination he began to drag himself in the direction of the nearest house hand over hand. He heard the sound of someone screaming, but he didn't recognize the strained voice as his own.

THE LAST STOP Bolan had scheduled for the evening was an old hotel on Fisher Avenue. The place had been abandoned and condemned some years earlier, but no one ever gotten around to leveling the structure. Vacant-windowed and graffiti-smeared, it was a kind of monument these days, much like the famous "Hotel Hell" staked out by runaways in Hollywood. Unlike its southern counterpart, however, this hulk—once the Fisher Arms—hadn't become a haven for the homeless. Rather, it was now a kind of home-away-from-home and part-time fortress for the Skulls.

It was a target the Executioner couldn't resist.

Approaching from the south on foot, he had no way of knowing in advance how many of his enemies would be inside. The place seemed dark at first, electric power cut off long ago, but if you stopped to let your eyes adjust, there was a faint, unstable light just visible in several of the windows—candlelight perhaps, or lanterns. Possibly an open fire for warmth.

He wore his blacksuit, skintight gloves and ski mask, with a military harness to support his web belt, side arm, extra magazines and hand grenades. The Uzi submachine gun slung across his shoulder had a foot-long silencer attached.

The chain-link fence around the Fisher Arms had gone to hell, along with every other aspect of the place. He had a dozen different slits to choose from on the south perimeter alone, where long incisions in the wire had left the fencing curled like parchment. Inside, the grass was six or seven inches high and filled with rustling life. He guessed that only changing seasons and incessant traffic kept the lawn from sprouting like a jungle and devouring the old hotel.

The fire escape was old and rusty, but it served his purpose. Bolan tested each step on the climb before proceeding, knowing that a sudden drop would pose more risk than broken bones, alerting members of the gang to an intruder on the grounds. He took his time and did it right, no hurry as his ears picked up the sounds of rap and soul from several different stereos inside.

Cool darkness greeted Bolan on the fourth floor as he slipped through a window. He double-checked the Uzi's safety, waiting for his eyes to make a new adjustment, finally picking out an open door about twenty-four feet away. On either side the new inhabitants had knocked out portions of the wall to form a runway through adjacent rooms.

The warrior reached the corridor, checking left and right before he moved in the direction of the stairs. He chose the downward path and let the Uzi lead him on his way.

And met a gang member coming up the stairs.

Against his better judgment Bolan gave the guy a choice, one instant hanging in the balance when he could have saved himself. Instead of bolting for his life, the young man cursed and thrust a hand inside his jacket to reach a hidden pistol. The movement sealed his fate.

The Uzi stuttered, the noise muffled by the silencer, and half a dozen Parabellum rounds struck home from fifteen feet away. Their impacts lifted Bolan's target off his feet and pitched him backward down the stairs, a hurtling rag doll leaving crimson smears across the filthy wall as he rebounded, slumping to the floor.

The Executioner kept moving, instinct taking over. He couldn't be sure if anyone downstairs had heard the shots or body impact, but he had no time to waste. On three he trailed music to a room where five Skulls and a couple of their female hangers-on were grooving to the sounds of rap.

He left the music playing, shouldering the Uzi for precision aim as he began to work the room from left to right. A thickset target first, his back turned, drawing on a joint when Bolan put the lights out with a 3-round burst. Next up, an agile dancer going through his moves, the slick routine disintegrated as a stream of Parabellum rounds mixed up the beat.

They saw him now, two runners breaking for the line of weapons stacked against a nearby wall. He caught them with a rising figure eight and saw them fall together, arms and legs entangled in a last embrace. The surviving Skull broke for cover toward a jagged hole that granted access to another room. The Uzi helped him get there with a burst between the shoulder blades, his body skimming facedown on a blood slick, coasting on a floor from which the inexpensive carpeting had long been peeled away.

The girls were frozen, staring at him, and he left them there. If either grabbed a piece and followed him, he'd confront the problem then. He wasn't prepared to execute two young women for their selection of companions.

He jogged back into the corridor as the girls began to scream. He met a Skull emerging from another room, two doors along, and dropped him where he stood.

Time was running out, the doomsday numbers falling in his mind.

Reloading on the move, he hit another flight of stairs and started down toward two. Below him angry-sounding voices picked out three or four potential targets, and he palmed a frag grenade, released the safety pin and leaned across the knife-scarred banister to let it drop.

The blast raised dust and screams of pain, the stairwell thick with smoke as Bolan started down. Two bodies crumpled on the landing, with a third six or seven yards away, all shrapnel-torn. A fourth was sitting with his back against the wall and screaming at his shattered legs when Bolan spent a mercy round to silence him.

It was the echo of the blast, he thought, that muffled running footsteps behind him on the stairs. He heard them too late, half turning as a body launched itself directly toward him, thin arms flung around his neck. He powered backward, slammed his enemy against the nearest wall and swung the Uzi's butt against a rack of scrawny ribs.

Long fingernails scraped Bolan's cheek and took the ski mask with them as his adversary tumbled to the floor. He trained the Uzi on a frightened, tear-streaked face and held his fire, choosing not to kill the unarmed girl.

But she'd seen him. It was time to go.

He was out a window, down the fire escape and across the yard before the first Skull started in pursuit, but there was no real contest to the chase.

Exposed.

How would the Skulls react now that they knew a white man had been gunning for them in their own backyard? As Bolan slid behind the rental's wheel and gunned away from there, he wondered if the shock might not be turned to his advantage with a little work.

It would be worth a try at least.

And in the last analysis he simply had no choice.

11

The pickets were in place by 9:00 a.m., parading up and down the sidewalk near the Skulls' clubhouse. A dozen of the enemy had lined up on the scruffy grass to curse and jeer, but police kept the two opposing sides apart. A boom box cranked up to the limit did its best to drown the chanting of the picketers, with their signs proclaiming Gangs Must Go, exhorting the authorities to Crack Down on Crack. A TV camera crew was working on the sidelines, shooting ten or fifteen minutes for a thirty-second spot on the evening news.

Vernon Souders led the parade, stepping out of line from time to time, urging on the faithful with a smile or encouraging word, facing the Skulls directly when he had the chance, determined not to be intimidated by their taunts and glares. These animals fed on fear, but Souders thought he could see behind the bright mask of bravado that they wore. He understood they were learning how to be afraid.

The game had been a one-way street in Hunters Point for much too long, the gang members strutting, showing off their guns and muscle, confident they were in control. The rival gangs were opposition, granted, but they could forget about police and the average citizens who populated neighborhoods like Hunters Point. Nobody cared at city hall, they reasoned, since the predators and their prey were all predominantly black. And by the time anyone wised up to the potential danger of the gangs, well, it would simply be too late.

The previous day's violence had changed all that, at least for the time being. Clustered on the grass and flashing obscene gestures with their hands, the Skulls looked as cocky as ever, but Souders picked up on a brand-new hint of insecurity he'd never felt from any member of the tribe before.

The man from Washington had done that, with his guns and God knows what. The grim events recorded in the morning paper had boggled Souders's mind, but he'd kept his mouth shut, hoping for the best.

The Skulls and Savage Nomads were reacting as anticipated. A few of the reports from last night's battle zone were obviously incidents involving group participation, with the triggermen identified as young black males. Civilian casualties were light, thank heavens, with a girl and two young men sustaining superficial wounds in separate incidents.

Where Blanski struck, by contrast, there was a unique precision to the work, with few survivors on the other side and no civilian dead or wounded in the lot. He seemed to balance out his strikes between the Skulls and Nomads, keeping up a kind of rhythm to the action, playing both sides off against the middle like a maestro.

One of the Skulls was shooting him the bird, and Souders stared him down, the young man muttering obscenities before he finally turned away. Another time, last week perhaps, it would have been impossible to undermine the young gangster's confidence.

Small favors.

Souders knew they were running out of time, whatever Blanski had in mind. The man from Washington couldn't afford to stretch his game too far beyond a point where time became the enemy. Between Skulls and Savage Nomads he'd been outnumbered about 150 guns to one when he began, and even with the casualties he'd inflicted up to this point, the odds were with the house. Toss in the hundreds of police who'd be scouring the streets with last night's mayhem fresh in mind, and Blanski would be skating on the very thinnest of thin ice.

And when he left, what then?

It was beyond the scope of any single man to wipe out all the gangs in San Francisco, and the Hunters Point he left behind would still be plagued with all the problems that allowed the gangs to take root in the first place. Poverty and broken families, an appetite for the escape that drugs provide—it was a neighborhood where life came cheap, and that would have to change.

That's our job, Souders thought, and fell back into line, his picket sign turned sideways so the few Skulls who could read would get the message loud and clear.

He saw the unmarked cruiser coming from a block away. Police departments spent a fortune on their vehicles, from motorcycles to the heavy armor used for raids and hostage situations, but the men who signed the purchase orders seemingly gave no thought whatsoever to variety. They seemed to think that slapping on a coat of brown or navy paint would magically disguise the standard four-door squad car, even when they left the rec lights in the window and the city plates attached.

So much for secrecy.

The cruiser parked across the street, and Captain Barney Gibson climbed out on the passenger side. He stood there for a moment, waiting until Souders met his gaze directly, then he beckoned with his hand.

Now what?

Souders fell out of line, hearing a new round of cat-calls from the Skulls as he crossed the street to speak with Captain Gibson. It wasn't about the picket line, he knew that much. The brass from Homicide wouldn't come down to chase some pickets off the sidewalk, even if the city was inclined to send them home.

Approaching Gibson's vehicle, he swallowed hard to clear the lump in his throat and concentrated on remaining calm.

THERE WERE ABOUT two dozen demonstrators on the picket line, three-quarters of them women old enough to have a child or two in school. It showed some nerve for them to face the Skulls this way, regardless of the bluesuit escort, when they knew a trigger-happy punk would stand at least a fifty-fifty chance of getting clean away if there was any trouble.

They had to be given credit, Gibson thought. He knew about disgust and how it built into anger over time, remaining locked inside until you either blew your top or found a channel of expression to relieve the pressure. Cops were known to suffer from the symptoms just like anybody else—and worse than most, which helped explain the odd stick-swinging melee now and then when someone cracked and let his anger stain the uniform.

This morning Barney Gibson just felt tired. Two hours of fitful sleep had left him feeling worse somehow than when he went to bed at half past four that morning. No new killings in the meantime, but he had a sneaking hunch they were standing in the eye of the storm, with another furious outburst preparing to sneak up and slap them from behind.

The trick was being ready when it came, watching all points of the compass at once and refusing to let yourself be surprised.

A nifty trick if you could pull it off.

He watched the pickets marching up and down for several moments, finally catching Vernon Souders's eye and waving him across the street. He watched the man approaching and wondered how much Souders knew.

He hadn't gotten into it with Bolan the previous night. Before they went their separate ways the Executioner assured him he was working on his own, and that was good enough for Gibson.

Still, he couldn't shake a feeling that the warrior had been summoned somehow, choosing San Francisco over New York City or other large cities with their more powerful, more lethal gangs. There had to be some kind of a connection, and he'd feel better knowing what it was.

"Good morning, Captain."

"You've got quite a turnout, Mr. Souders."

"A citizens' response to last night's violence, Captain. We appreciate the escort, by the way."

"It doesn't have a thing to do with me. If you ask my opinion, I'd be bound to say you're courting trouble."

"We already have the trouble," Souders said. "No courting necessary. The fact is, we're inviting it to leave."

"Good luck."

"I'm hoping for a little more than that."

The captain frowned. "Such as?"

"With all the bloodshed in the past twenty-four hours, perhaps some action from authorities. It might be tardy, but it's not too late."

"We're working on it," Gibson told him honestly. "These cases don't exactly leave us with a ton of evidence or willing witnesses."

"In that case I wish luck to you."

"It couldn't hurt."

"Well, if there's nothing else..."

"Hang on a second, will you? Yesterday when I was at your house you said you made a call to Washington."

"That's right."

"And there was no response at all?"

"More like a kiss-off, I suppose you'd say. I got a call back, but they weren't encouraging. Some kind of double-talk and legalese I didn't understand."

"Who did you talk to?" Gibson asked.

"I really couldn't say."

"Would the name 'Blanski' ring a bell, by any chance?"

Souders missed a beat, but he was cool about it, covering with a pretense of thought before he shook his head in an emphatic negative. "I'm sorry, no. I really can't remember, but I don't think that was it."

"Okay, just checking."

"Checking what?"

"I guess it won't surprise you if I say the brass is on my back to clear up these shootings. It crossed my mind that if the Feds had something going on the side, well, maybe..."

Souders shook his head again, no hesitation this time. "Sorry, Captain. If I thought I could help you..."

"Never mind. It was a long shot, anyway."

He watched as Souders made his way back to the picket line and fell in step behind a woman in a lime-green pantsuit. On the grass the Skulls were slapping hands and nudging one another, grinning like the guests of honor at a party whipped up by the mayor. As Gibson stood and watched, he felt a sudden urge to cross the street and slap the gloating smiles right off their faces, keep on pounding until there was nothing left but silence and submission.

Get a grip, he warned himself.

A lot of good that did. The public wanted tough cops when the plague of crime hit close to home, but you were still supposed to be professional about it, guarding everybody's rights against abuse and making sure no one put a knot on John Doe's head because he was caught dealing drugs to kids in elementary school. It got a little weird, protecting everyone at once, but that was how they wrote the rules.

Until Mack Bolan had come along and started slipping in amendments, right.

Small wonder that a number of detectives down the line had closed their eyes to Bolan's actions when the guy blew into town. He was disruptive, sure as hell, but so was any sudden storm that blew the garbage and accumulated filth away.

If you were smart, you just hung on and let it blow.

Or maybe, if you had a chance, you helped direct the store.

"Let's go," he told his driver, fastening the seat belt around his ample waist.

"Where to?"

"We've seen the Skulls," Gibson said. "Let's go take a gander at the Nomads."

"Alone?"

"Don't sweat it, Frank. I have a feeling they'll be cool."

"I WISH THOSE PIGS would take a coffee break," Weed muttered, staring out the window with a grim look on his face.

"No problem," One Shot told his number two. "We know these people from the neighborhood. They won't be going far."

"We ought to pay 'em back sometime."

"There's time and time," the leader of the Skulls replied. "Right now we got a more important problem."

He was thinking of the unknown white man who had trashed their compound hours earlier and wiped out nearly a dozen of his people in the process. Military threads and hardware all the way, which made him think that maybe he was premature in blaming the Savage Nomads for the crack house on Arleta. With a honkie in the woodpile, maybe both of them were being had.

It was a righteous plan, the more he thought about it. Building on the well-known hate between the Skulls and Nomads, it would only take a little pressure here, a small nudge there, to have them at each other's throats. Some kind of fucking grade-A brainstorm, but his grudging admiration wouldn't tell him who had conceived the plan.

Rule out the Nomads first, since they were getting hit as hard—or harder—than the Skulls. Another gang perhaps, but One Shot couldn't picture any of the homeboys taking on a honkie shooter when they could have put their own man in a ski mask just as easily. The stoner gangs were white, okay, but they were also mostly wimps without the nerve or necessary cash to mount an operation of this scale.

One thing the leader of the Skulls was sure about—you couldn't hire a shooter of this quality, with military hardware out the ass, unless you laid out major bread. He thought of the Sicilians and immediately ruled them out. They were a bunch of gray-haired has-beens, eating their spaghetti while they blew a lot of gas about the good old days when they were still on top.

And who was left?

He watched the pickets marching up and down, imagining how easy it would be to hose them with a burst of automatic fire and watch them drop. The mental picture made him smile, but he didn't relax. Too much to think about, and he was getting nowhere fast.

He followed Vernon Souders with his eyes, a new thought sparking in his mind. The old man was supposed to be some kind of combat vet or something. He might have buddies from the old days, maybe even contacts with the Feds that he could call on in a pinch. If he got pissed enough or pushed the panic button, could he count on GI Joe to lend a hand?

The warlord of the Skulls suspected he was getting paranoid, but what the hell? A little paranoia didn't hurt when there were people out to kill you every day. It would be stupid *not* to think he had enemies when he could rattle off the names of ten or fifteen other gangs at least that would have gladly paid to see him dead.

And what about Souders? Granted, they'd tried to dust him off some months ago, and muffed the job. He'd been chosen for the drive-by since he acted as a mouthpiece for the neighborhood, forever raising hell about the gangs. A piece of shit like that, you had to take him down or he was in your face forever, making others think they could defy the family and walk away without a scratch.

That kind of thing was bad for business, and it had to be squashed early on.

They should have followed up and done it right, but that was hindsight, and it hadn't seemed important at the time. A second run on Souders would have brought down too much heat just then, and One Shot had allowed himself to think their point had been made. The old man took it easy, for a little while, but then he started acting up again . . . and here they were.

He couldn't picture Souders taking on a hired gun, but you never could tell. The main thing was, he couldn't think of anybody else at all who might have brought a white man in to try to stir up a gang war.

If Souder *was* to blame, he had a lesson coming, and a notion was already forming in the back of Johnson's mind. But first he had to cut his losses if he could, cool his action with the Nomads for a bit and let the heat die down.

There would be time though for screwing Playboy Raymond by and by after the present shitstorm blew away. Right now it seemed to Johnson that they had a common enemy, and he was using them like puppets, yanking on their strings.

"We got a number for the Playboy?"

Weed was momentarily confused. "Phone number?"

"Yeah."

"We used to. I can check."

"You do that, cuz. I got some things to tell the man."

12

Bolan told himself it could have been worse. Leaving the girl alive was a judgment call, but it was done now. He didn't regret the choice, although it jeopardized his strategy to play the gangs off against each other, pushing them toward a final clash that would destroy them both.

The ball was rolling now, and even when the word began to spread among the Skulls that one of their assailants was a white man, they'd still have other problems. The morning news told Bolan that the gangs were wading in with everything they had, and there were half a dozen shootings overnight in which he had no part.

For now, a white assailant might provide an extra twist to keep the gangs off balance, trying to decide how they should prosecute their war. They had no hope of making Bolan, even with a fair description of his face, and Barney Gibson was the only one so far who knew the Executioner was back in town.

He thought of touching base with Gibson, but the radio and morning paper told him everything he had to know about the progress of his strategy. With Bolan's help the gangs had set a one-night record for fatalities, and there was apprehension that the list of dead would grow before the day was out.

A safe bet, Bolan thought.

Four hours' sleep in a motel off Highway 101 had helped with the fatigue. A shower left him feeling clean, if not exactly fresh, and breakfast in the coffee shop was passable. He had his checklist on the seat beside him when he hit the streets.

The best way Bolan knew of coping with an unexpected problem was to turn the thing around and use it to his own advantage if he could. As far as he could tell, the Skulls were conscious of a white man being linked to their misfortune, but the Savage Nomads would be ignorant of new developments. It was an angle he could work with if he played his cards correctly in the next few hours.

The notes from Vernon Souders listed several names for ranking officers in each gang, with a home address where information was available. It must have taken time, collecting information on the different gangs, and Bolan knew it hadn't been done without substantial risk. He scanned the list, ignoring the commanders for the moment, searching out a likely prospect for the brand-new game he had in mind—and found him, with a brief description of his duties with the gang.

It was a gamble, but the same was true of almost every move Bolan made from day to day. If he could sell the story to his one-man audience, the impact would recoup whatever damage he'd suffered in the raid the previous night, and he might still wind up ahead.

He drove north on Highway 101 to Third Street, branching off on Underwood and circling back toward Hunters Point. It would be somewhat different this time, going in without a coverall disguise, but he was counting on the suit and nondescript sedan to help him out.

The dealer's name was Raford Tucker, but he went by "Candy Man" when he was working on the street. The Nomads who had ever known his given name would long since have forgotten it, a thing of no importance in their world.

The crash pad was a loft on Robinson, and Bolan parked in a nearby alley, waiting for his mark to surface. Twenty minutes later Candy Man emerged, a face familiar to the warrior from the mug shots he'd picked up on his visit to the Hall of Justice.

Bingo.

Bolan trailed his mark for half a block before he curbed the car, leaned across the seat and opened the passenger door.

"Good morning, Raford."

"What do you want, man?"

"Have a seat."

"Fuck you."

The sight of the Beretta changed his mind, and Tucker slid into the car.

"This has got to be a roust."

The car was in motion as the Executioner replied, "No roust. I've got a message for Playboy. You're delivering."

"Says who?"

The pistol nudged his ribs.

"I've got this sneaking hunch you'll see things my way."

"Hey, I might at that."

"It's simple. Playboy Raymond and the Nomads have been set up for the kill."

"What else is new? The fuckin' Scumbags have been workin' overtime to dust us for the past two years."

"New game. They're using outside talent on the job this time."

"I'm sure."

"I don't care squat if you believe it, Raford. All you have to do is pass the word."

"Who *are* you, man?"

"The outside talent. I do a job, I figure payment's due upon delivery, okay? Somebody tries to stiff me, all the bets are off."

"You're telling me the Scumbags owe you money?"

"Fifty large so far. Another fifty when I hand them Raymond's head."

"And now you're blowing it?"

"*They* blew it. Midnight was the deadline, and I don't believe in unpaid overtime."

"So why tell me?"

"I thought it might be worth a little something to the Nomads, knowing what goes on. Kick in a bonus, and I might just be available to turn the game around."

"We're doin' fine just as it is."

"I'll make a note. Meanwhile, why don't we let the man in charge decide?"

"No harm in passing on the word, I guess."

"My thoughts exactly."

Bolan pulled in to the curb once more. The whole exchange had taken just three blocks.

"That's it?" Candy Man inquired.

"You're out of here."

"Say, what's your name in case somebody wants to know?"

"No names. I'll get in touch."

A lazy shrug. "Hey, suit yourself."

Bolan left the dealer standing curbside, staring after him until the morning traffic got between them, cutting off his view.

It was a start at least, but he couldn't be sure where it would lead. If nothing else, at least he'd have sown some more confusion in the hostile ranks.

"I'M TELLIN' YOU," Candy Man repeated, "a white dude grabs me off the street and sticks a fuckin' cannon in my face. Says I'm supposed to take a message back to Playboy Raymond unless I want to die."

The leader of the Savage Nomads lit another cigarette and scowled through curling smoke. "Go on."

"So, anyway, we take a ride, about two, three blocks. It didn't take him long to run it down."

"This white dude told you he was workin' for the Scumbags?"

Candy Man nodded, putting on an earnest face. "That's what he said. Tells me One Shot promised fifty large for what he did so far, and fifty more for wastin' you. They turn around and stiffed him on the first part, so he's pissed."

"This white dude be the one who hit us yesterday?"

"I didn't ask him that. Could be, I guess. The fucker's cool enough."

"He look like pork to you?"

Candy Man considered it and finally shook his head. "Suit wasn't cheap enough," he answered, "and the piece he showed me wasn't no pig iron."

"What kind of piece?"

"It looked like a Beretta, man, but there was somethin' funny. All I know, it had a big ol' fuckin' clip."

"The thing I ask myself is, how come he didn't blow you up?"

"I told you, man, he's pissed off at the Scumbags now. Dude wanted me to carry word that they been runnin' down."

"Why you?"

"Say what?"

"How come this white dude out of nowhere picks you out to be his mouthpiece if you never saw his ass before? I mean, how come he even knows where you be hangin' out?"

Candy Man looked nervous now. He saw where this was going, and he didn't like the drift. He had a choice, and running scared wasn't the way to go if he intended to survive the afternoon.

"You think I'm shittin' you? I make this bullshit up and come in here for what, so you can get pissed off and whack my ass? What kind of fool do you think I am?"

The warlord of the Savage Nomads thought about it for a moment and decided that it made no sense. Candy Man wasn't a hero-type, and he wouldn't improve his status in the gang by swinging their attention from the Skulls to some imaginary white man in the middle of a shooting war. It stood to reason, therefore, that his story was the truth—but that didn't resolve the nagging doubts in Playboy Raymond's mind.

"Nobody's saying you're lyin'," he replied at length. "The question is, how come this total stranger went to you?"

"I don't know how he found me, man. Same way he found the brothers he iced, I wouldn't be surprised. Dude checks things out before he makes a move."

"So what's he want from us?"

"He didn't ask for anything. I got the feeling he was warnin' us to pay the Scumbags back or maybe screw around with something they got in mind."

"Like, if we know they set a white dude up to hit us. We'd be ready when they pull some other shit?"

"Like that."

"That's it?"

"Dude said he might get back in touch if there was somethin' else."

"Okay. Take off."

There were degrees of mental acumen among the Savage Nomads. Playboy Raymond was among the sharper members of the gang in terms of street smarts, but he wouldn't be confused with Einstein on the best day he ever had. A functional illiterate who had failed his freshman courses twice before he'd taken the hint and hung it up, he ran the gang as much on nerve and muscle as on brains. It didn't bother him to know that people hated him and longed to see him dead; that came with being in a gang. The scary part was the idea of someone thinking overtime of ways to do him in. He wasn't sure exactly how to counter that before it got him killed.

"Okay," he told the empty room, "stay cool. It'll all work out just fine."

"Hey, cuz?"

He swiveled in his chair and frowned at T-Bone, waiting in the doorway. It was getting so that he couldn't have a goddamn minute to himself these days. "What is it?"

"You okay, man?"

"Fine." A trace of irritation showed in his voice. "What's happening?"

"You got a phone call," T-Bone answered. "Dude says he's One Shot Johnson, and he wants a meet."

13

"Remember, I want everybody on their toes, you dig?"

"I hear you, man," Weed answered, navigating through traffic.

"I mean it," One Shot Johnson warned, getting nervous and despising the emotion for the weakness it implied.

"No sweat."

Behind him, sitting in the back end of the van, six homeboys met his gaze and nodded solemnly, all armed and ready to defend their number one if it came down to that.

The meet was set for neutral ground, with each side bringing seven men besides the warlord. He'd been a bit surprised when Playboy Raymond went along with the idea, and neither one had bothered to suggest they should leave their guns at home. A man would have to be an idiot to sit down with his mortal enemies and not be packing iron.

The van belonged to Weed's first cousin, and they had righteous papers in the glove compartment if they got pulled over by the police. Weed held it to the posted limit, rolling west on Northridge, picking up the loop on Ingalls to La Salle.

The meeting was a gamble, but One Shot knew they could win the jackpot if he pulled it off. His conversation on the phone with Playboy was the first time they'd talked in more than eighteen months, and Johnson kept it short. He didn't mention anything about the white dude or the possibility that someone on the outside of the gangs was trying to manipulate their feud. He had a feeling Playboy Raymond would have laughed at him and hung up, but he would have to listen when it went down face-to-face.

Once more he thought about the possibility that he was making a mistake. Suppose the Nomads sent a couple of dozen soldiers to the park and tried to smoke his ass? It was a risk that came with leadership, but he'd made his choice and he'd follow through. If nothing else, he knew Playboy Raymond's troops were being hit as often and as badly as the Skulls. So far he figured the game was more or less a draw, and they'd both be looking for a way to disengage while saving face. He understood what the ritual involved and thought his news about the white dude might be what the doctor ordered.

Not that he expected Playboy Raymond and the Nomads to accept his word, first thing. They'd be cautious going in, mistrusting everything he said, reluctant to concede they were hurting from the hits they'd taken. It would require diplomacy to pull it off, and while the spoken word had never been his strong suit, Johnson thought he could make the sale.

And if he did, what then?

His first idea, a coalition to defeat the common enemy, might not go down so well, but he was bound to try. If nothing else, he had a temporary cease-fire on his mind, just long enough to tag the honkie dude and prove his point. That done, his own position would be

doubly enhanced, within the Skulls and in the estimation of his enemies.

Not bad if he could swing it, but he still had numer-
ous unanswered questions preying on his mind. Who
was this white man, anyway? What had prompted him
to turn against the gangs and start a shooting war? Was
he official, some weird kind of superpig, or were there
private elements at work?

Worse yet, suppose it turned out he was working for
the Nomads, and they knew about him all along?

No good.

By One Shot's calculation, Playboy Raymond's
clique had suffered three or four attacks for which the
Skulls weren't responsible. In every case where witnesses survived, the shooter was supposed to be one
guy, some kind of Rambo-type who fitted the white
dude's style. That made it plain he was playing both
ends off against the middle, working on some program
of his own.

They didn't even need to think about what Whitey
had in mind right now. The first thing was to stop him
cold before he did more damage to the family. If they
could capture him alive and run some questions by him,
great. If not, then Johnson would be satisfied to see him
lying stretched out on the pavement, cold and dead. A
little luck and they could finish it, assuming he was on
his own. And if somebody else was waiting in the shadows, calling the shots, they'd be smart enough to see
they couldn't fuck around with One Shot Johnson and
the Skulls.

Once Whitey took his dive, there would be ample
time for dealing with the Nomads by the numbers, just
as they'd done before. If everything was cool, a cease-
fire might convince Playboy and his homeys to relax,

and that was all the edge Johnson needed for a swift, clean sweep.

He felt the tension easing in his neck a little, and he looked forward to the meeting now that he'd mapped it in his mind. It didn't matter if Playboy tried to throw a curve or two his way, since One Shot would be ready for him, marking time and looking fine.

And if it all went to hell, he had seven of his best guns standing by to kick some ass before they all went down in flames.

The one thing you never counted on when you were running with the gangs was growing old. Some mornings Johnson woke up knowing he was short on time, an old man by the standard of the streets. Many of his friends were dead or rotting in a cell, and it made him feel like something of a curiosity to be up still and walking underneath the open sky.

If this turned out to be the day he bit the big one, he was ready for it, and he damn sure wouldn't go alone. If he survived and sold his program to the Nomads, he'd be well on his way to earning status as a gangland legend.

It would be a toss-up. He could make history or be history, two sides of a coin that was already spinning in midair. Whichever way it landed, One Shot Johnson was prepared.

"THEY'RE HERE," T-Bone announced, standing up and tugging on his jacket so the Uzi wouldn't show so much.

"Okay, look sharp."

It all came down to this, Playboy Raymond thought, standing in the park with seven men behind you, waiting for the enemy to speak his piece or make his move. The Ingram submachine gun was a deadweight at his side, suspended from his shoulder by a length of nylon twine. The right-hand pocket of his raincoat had been slit to let him reach the little stuttergun more quickly, swing it out and let it rip before his opposition even knew they were dead.

A part of Raymond hoped it would go that way, a chance to make one swift, decisive strike against his enemies and let the Savage Nomads take their rightful place as leaders of the pack. Yet another part of him was sweating, hoping there was some way they could chill it out before he lost another dozen men and wound up with a gang cut back to half its starting size. Right now he had the peewees lined up, begging for a chance to join, but it was bad for business and morale, so many funerals at once.

The van his opposition drove stopped twenty feet away against the curb. Playboy watched the Skulls unloading, dressed much like his own men, with their jackets meant to cover hardware even though the day was warm.

"You wouldn't have a couple more inside there, would you?" Playboy asked.

One Shot Johnson let the insult slide without a blink. "You went to check it out?"

"I trust you, man."

They both knew *that* was bullshit, but it sounded nice. If there were angry words to come, he meant to let the Scumbags start it off.

"It's good you came," Johnson said.

Playboy shrugged. "You said it was important. We're listening."

"There's somethin' you should know about the shit's been goin' on since yesterday."

"Such as?"

"Some of the hits you took, we never made," the warlord of the Skulls replied. "We didn't snipe your place, for instance, and we didn't burn down your warehouse."

"You say."

"I didn't figure you'd believe me, so I'll ask you straight. You waste our crack house on Arleta? Did you bust our place on Fisher Avenue?"

"We might've," Playboy answered. "Might've not."

"I'm bettin' not. You maybe *wish* you did, but some white dude got there ahead of you and did the job."

Playboy felt a prickling of his scalp. He didn't even risk a glance at T-Bone, standing by his side. "White dude?"

"You heard me right."

He forced a crooked smile. "Sounds like you been smokin' what you should be sellin' on the street."

"Fact is, he popped our digs on Fisher last night, late. I lost more men than I can spare right now, but he got careless with a bitch who tore his ski mask off and let her live. She saw his face. You follow what I'm tellin' you?"

"I heard you," Playboy said. "It doesn't mean you're going to lead me anywhere."

A careless shrug from Johnson. "If that's the way you want it, fine. I don't mind fightin' both of you at once if that's how it goes. Just thought you'd want to know the skinny, so you don't be wastin' time on payback for a bunch of shit we never done."

"How am I supposed to know this ain't a lot of bullshit?"

"I already told you that," One Shot replied. "Both of us are standin' here and knowin' you didn't make the hits I just ran down. That means somebody else has been cappin' on the Skulls, and on your people, too.''

"Who says it has to play that way? Somebody else hits you a couple of times, it don't mean he's after me.''

"It does if he's been usin' both of us against the other, startin' something the two of us'll have to finish on our own.''

"How come?''

"I don't have all the answers, man. I just know what I know.''

"Be cool now,'' Playboy cautioned, reaching underneath his jacket from the front to lift the Ingram out. He handed it to T-Bone, waiting while his first lieutenant tucked the weapon out of sight. "Let's take a walk.''

"Suits me.''

The warlord of the Skulls produced a sawed-off 12-gauge pump and passed it to the one called Weed. He fell in step at Raymond's side, and they began to walk in the direction of the swings a hundred yards away.

"You know Candy Man?'' Raymond asked, gambling everything.

"I heard the name.''

"He's one of mine. Came to see me this morning with a story about some honkie who grabbed him off the street like it was nothin', showin' him a gun and all.''

"I'm listening.''

"Thing is, this honkie said he used to work for you. Says you promised fifty large to take the Nomads down, and now you're holdin' out. He tips us off because he's pissed and wants to get you back.''

"That's total bullshit, man.''

"There was supposed to be another fifty large for me alone.''

"You swallow that? I'd rather take and wipe my ass with fifty large than pay some white dude for a job I could do myself."

Playboy let it pass, intent on reading Johnson's face and tone. He wasn't any kind of TV psychic, but he *was* a decent judge of character, and he didn't believe Johnson had the brains to put him on.

There was too much coincidence in the leader of the Skulls cooking up a tale about a white dude just when Candy Man checked in with his report. There was an outside chance that One Shot knew his soldier was defecting, maybe hoped he could minimize the damage with a lie, but it was thin.

For starters, Raymond knew his people hadn't scorched the Fisher Arms, much less the crack house on Arleta Avenue. And if *they* hadn't . . .

"So let's say I buy it. What's the deal?"

"I did some thinkin'," One Shot told him, as if it were some kind of miracle. "Here's what we do. . . ."

THE CALL FROM Gang Intervention was an annoyance, but Barney Gibson could hardly ignore it under the circumstances. He agreed to meet Earl Weathers in the Hall of Justice cafeteria at noon and kept his fingers crossed.

His worry was that Weathers might have stumbled onto something that would tip him off to Bolan's presence in the city. Gibson was already pushing it, withholding information on his own and watching out for anything that surfaced in the homicide investigations he was handling, but he had no pull at all with GIU. It was a fact that he outranked Lieutenant Weathers, but the GIU commander answered to a different captain, and there would be hell to pay if Gibson tried to throw his weight around between divisions.

Still, it didn't have to be a lead on Bolan, and the more he thought about it, Gibson was convinced it must be something else—some rumble from the gangland underground perhaps that Weathers meant to pass along, a gesture of cooperation on the case.

Okay. He'd relax and hear what Weathers had to say before he started worrying. The odds were, it was nothing new at all. More likely, GIU was checking in and hoping for an update on the progress of the homicide investigation.

Right.

The cafeteria was filling up when Gibson got there. He bought a cup of coffee and found a table near the door where he could watch for Weathers coming in.

The GIU lieutenant showed five minutes later and headed straight to Gibson's table, where he took a seat.

"Not eating?" Gibson asked.

"Brown bag. How about yourself?"

"Can't seem to find my appetite today. What's up?"

"You know I cultivate some snitches in the gangs." It didn't come out sounding like a question.

"Sure, I figured. Do they give you much?"

Weathers shrugged. "Mostly gossip, with a twist in favor of the clique they represent. Somebody shot somebody else, but it was all the victim's fault, that kind of thing. It's not much good for bringing charges, but it helps me keep a finger on the pulse."

"I hear you," Gibson said. "When I was on the harbor watch, it seemed like half the stevedores in town were calling up and fingering some guy they didn't like for everything from petty theft to murder and extortion. Most of it was crap, but we picked up some decent information on the unions now and then."

"The thing is," Weathers told him, "I got something bigger just before I called you. Say an hour back. One of my snitches in the Savage Nomads tells me the warlords had a face-to-face in Hilltop Park this morning, working on a truce."

A frown creased Gibson's face. "They're knocking off? What was it—too much heat?"

The GIU lieutenant shook his head. "My caller didn't have it all, you understand, but he's been catching whispers through the grapevine all day long. The gist is, the Skulls and Nomads might be closing ranks against a common enemy."

A sudden chill stiffened the hairs on Gibson's nape. "Say what?"

"You heard me right. They seem to think somebody else pulled off at least a couple of hits before it really started rolling. Rumor in the ranks is that it's a white man, maybe working for the Mafia."

The captain felt a tingling in his stomach that would soon become a full-fledged burn. "I guess you buzzed the special unit up on this?"

"First thing," Weathers replied. "They made me feel like I was playing with myself, okay? Point A, they've got the local Family covered, so the Don can't take a crap without somebody getting it on tape. Point B, the gangs have had no opposition from the Mob these past two years, so why should they expect a firefight now? Point C, the unit has more pressing matters on its mind, like tracing bank accounts and logging stolen TV sets the Family hijacked out of Dipshit, West Virginia. It's like talking to a wall."

"You think it's the Sicilians?"

Weathers frowned. "I don't know who it is. Hell, I'm not even saying there *is* some white guy out there kicking ass. My source might be all wrong, or maybe he's been listening to someone who's got shit for brains. I just thought someone ought to know, and maybe check it out."

"I'll do that," Gibson told him. "Anyway, I'll try. Gang members aren't much on sharing information with 'the pigs,' and we're a little short of uninvolved civilian witnesses."

"Like always."

"I still appreciate the tip. If it comes to anything, we'll cosign the report, so you get credit for your work."

"The collar isn't on my mind right now. You'll laugh, but after working GIU a while, you start to care about these kids. Some of them, anyway. Hell, I know lots of them are hopeless, and we need to throw away the key. There's some I'd pull the switch on myself if they were in the green rooms, okay? But others, well, I get the feeling they could use a break, that's all. It's not my job, but I just want to lift them out of there and show them there's a better way to live."

"Good luck."

"No luck so far. You ever feel like you were bailing out the goddamn ocean with a shot glass?"

"Every day," Gibson said, meaning it.

"Me, too."

"So, anyway, I'll keep in touch on anything we find that might relate. If you hear any more about this Mr. X, I wouldn't mind a tip."

"You got it. Is the coffee any good?"

"That depends. You have a car that needs the paint stripped off?"

"I get the idea. I'll pass."

"Good choice."

He watched the GIU lieutenant go, allowing Weathers time to clear the floor before he left the cafeteria and headed for the elevators. Gibson told himself it was nothing, just some gas an informant had passed along, but, on the other hand...

If it was true that the gangs were closing ranks, the shift could easily take Bolan by surprise. The Executioner was slick, no doubt about it, but without a tip he'd continue plotting moves as if the gangs were still at war with each other, correspondingly oblivious to any outside threat. It would be easier that way for Bolan's opposition to devise a trap and maybe even catch him unaware.

All right.

He knew the problem; it was the solution that eluded Barney Gibson at the moment. He couldn't look up Bolan in the phone book under *E* for Executioner and leave a message on his answering machine. There might be someone, somewhere, who was capable of touching base, but Gibson didn't have the first idea how to get in touch with them. Which meant that he'd have to wait, and maybe keep his fingers crossed for luck.

The burning in his stomach was a full-blown conflagration now, and there was nothing he could do about it. Nothing but continue going through the motions of his job... and wait.

14

The check-in was a mere formality at first. The Homicide division would have better sources on the street, and Bolan didn't like proceeding blindly where he had a chance to scrutinize the enemy before he moved. Deployment, strengths and weaknesses, morale—it all went into the successful preparation of campaigns.

He used a pay phone near the Silver Terrace Playground and asked for Captain Gibson, working homicide.

"Who's calling, please?"

"Mike Bradley. I'm with the *Examiner*."

"Okay, hang on."

It was a simple ruse, and probably a waste of time, but he couldn't rule out some effort at a trace. If Gibson underwent a change of heart and let them have the "Blanski" name, at least this trick should throw them off until he had the captain on the line. And if the game was going sour, Bolan thought he could pick it up in Gibson's voice.

"Hello?"

"What's new?"

"Well, damn. They told me it was some guy from the media."

"I've never been much good at holding down a job."

"I'm glad you called."

"Why's that?"

"Not here. You feel like having lunch?"

"I think I've lost my appetite," the soldier told him, smelling trouble.

"You can fake it. How about Balboa Park on San José."

"You've got a thing for parks these days."

"Just call me nature boy."

"How long?"

"I have to clean up some things here before I leave. Let's say an hour."

"Fine."

"And, hey, if it was me, I'd mellow out until we talk, okay?"

"I'll see what I can do."

"One hour."

Gibson severed the connection, Bolan cutting off the dial tone as he dropped the handset into its cradle. There was something in the captain's tone that set his teeth on edge, but what the hell?

Another game of wait-and-see. It was a risk he ran whenever public servants started rubbing shoulders with his war. He wasn't worried that the homicide detective would attempt to set him up or take control of the campaign, per se, but he'd have to bide his time and judge the latest crisis for himself.

Returning to his car, he found the ramp for interstate 280 near the playground, following the traffic westbound toward the cutoff for the city college and Balboa Park. He took his time, no hurry with an hour left to kill, and made a thorough recon of the neighborhood before he parked his car near the exit of the public lot.

Whatever happened next, they wouldn't take him by surprise.

There hadn't been an opportunity as yet to follow up on his discussion with Candy Man. The latest bulletins on radio revealed no further flare-ups in the war between the Skulls and Nomads, but he didn't want to press his luck by moving in again too soon. He'd provide a little time for them to stew perhaps before he launched the next offensive in a bid to keep them at each other's throat.

It bothered Bolan when he had to let his enemies step back and gain their second wind, but there were times when interruptions to the blitzing schedule couldn't be avoided, times when he could only wait and let the seeds he'd planted sprout and grow inside suspicious minds.

There was a chance the pissed-off mercenary angle might not sell with One Shot Johnson and the Skulls, but he was playing it by ear. If nothing else, the warlord's paranoia would be aggravated, leaving him to wonder what the hell was going on. His hatred for the Savage Nomads was a matter of established fact, the two gangs locked in combat as it was, and he was banking on their enmity to light the fuse. Unless...

He blanked his mind deliberately, refusing to be sidetracked by hypotheses of failure. Gibson would be with him shortly, and the homicide detective would relay his news. From that point on it would be Bolan's job to settle on a fitting course of action, nudge the game into its final round and wrap things up as best he could.

No problem.

The tricky part was getting out alive.

AFTER FOUR HOURS on the picket line, Vernon Souders thought they'd made their point. The television cameras had withdrawn an hour earlier, content with their accumulated footage, ready to go back and trim it down to ten or fifteen seconds for the evening news.

If that much, Souders thought, aware that news was transitory at the best of times. Another shooting or a gruesome pileup on the interstate could push his pickets off the tube entirely, relegating them to minor items in the daily press.

It wouldn't be a waste of time, regardless. Not in Souders's mind at least. He hadn't joined this fight for the publicity, but rather viewed the newsmen as a tool to help him put new pressure on the gangs. Despite their reputations for audacious acts of violence, hoodlums thrived on secrecy, their business best conducted in the dark of night, away from prying eyes. If he could mobilize a larger segment of the neighborhood by publicizing who the Skulls and Nomads were, then it was worth the effort and the risk involved.

Souders made another pass in front of the assembled Skulls and stepped out of the line. He raised a hand, the others pausing in their march along the sidewalk, watching him.

"I think we've made our point," he told them, noting disappointment on a couple of the faces, frank relief on others. "I appreciate your turning out this way on such short notice. Each and every one of you, I want to thank you for your help."

A few of them were smiling now, signs lowered as they started drifting toward their cars. Behind them on the grass the Skulls were watching, letting out new catcalls at the enemy's retreat.

"'Bout time y'all got smart and went back home," one of the gang members shouted.

"If you poke your nose where it ain't supposed to be," another called, "you might not have a home to go to."

"Fuckin' candy-ass crusaders."

That voice sounded closer, and Souders turned just in time to catch a flash of movement in the corner of his eye. A slender youth was veering away from him in the direction of the nearest pickets, one fist cocked to strike. "Look out!" Souders cried.

But the warning was too late. The attacker struck a woman from behind, her legs turning to rubber as she slumped at the curb. Her husband swung around, fists clenched, a glint of sudden hatred in his eyes.

A patrolman got there first and seized the young man in a painful hammerlock, half dragging him across the street and slamming him against a squad car, where his hands were cuffed behind his back. The woman was already on her feet, a little dazed, her husband and a second officer beside her, asking questions.

"Grace, are you all right?"

"I'm fine. A little shaken up is all."

"You're sure."

"I'm sure."

The policeman looked at the woman. "Ma'am, if you'd be interested in pressing charges for assault..."

"You bet your life I would."

Souders let them go, aware there was nothing he could say. It was a minor incident, perhaps an hour's headache, and the punk would certainly be free on bond before the afternoon was out.

"Old man!"

This time when Souders turned around he recognized the face. Officially he didn't know the warlord of the Skulls; their paths had never crossed, and they hadn't been introduced, but Souders had reviewed a stack of mug shots at the Hall of Justice and his memory was excellent.

"What is it, Elroy?" He knew it would anger the warlord to hear his given name.

"You know me, huh? That's good. We know each other now."

"You've got your jackals punching women from behind," Souders said. "I guess he must have left his pistol home today."

"I told 'em to keep hands off," Johnson said, putting on a frown. "Could be I have to kick his ass when he gets out."

"If you need some help, feel free to call."

"That's pretty good. You're one tough old man, I guess."

"I'm not afraid of you if that's what's on your mind."

"What's on my mind is tellin' you we know about your game, okay?"

"What game is that?"

"Play dumb if you want to. I don't mind. I *know,* okay?"

"This isn't going anywhere."

He was about to turn away when Johnson caught his arm. After a glance at the restraining hand, and another bluesuit moving closer, he felt himself released.

"If you want to play some wise-ass game with me," the warlord hissed, "you ought to know what's on the table. Fuck around with how I live, you might lose everything you got."

"I wouldn't think some signs would make you all that nervous, Elroy."

"Fuck the signs, okay? If old bitches need some time out of the house, I don't care if they march up and down the goddamn street all night. You try to take me off, that's somethin' else."

"Your paranoia's showing."

"Maybe so. We'll see who's paranoid come payback time."

"I don't respond to threats."

"A smart old man like you should recognize a promise when he hears one," Johnson said, the sneering smile back on his face. "When you start a war with me, I finish it."

"We'll see."

"That's right, old man. Remember where you heard it first."

He turned away from Elroy Johnson, walking slowly toward his car. A number of the other pickets were already gone, the last few waiting by their vehicles to see him safely off. A squad car lingered at the scene until the last of them had driven out of sight.

As Souders drove, he pondered Johnson's words. The young man had been angry, but he didn't sound like someone who was blustering, without some weight behind his words.

I know, okay?

Know what?

It clicked for Souders then, and almost took him off the road. Blanski. What else could the warlord of the Skulls have meant?

Dear God.

The question raised a host of others, crowding in on one another fast and furious. How had the secret been revealed? Was Johnson guessing, or had he collected evidence? What had he meant exactly with the reference to "payback time"?

The gangs had tried to murder Vernon Souders twice, and they'd failed each time. That didn't mean they'd give up trying, but the slowest moron learned from his mistakes in time.

But if they tried another angle of attack . . .

His hands locked on the steering wheel. Sweet Jesus! "Corey."

He was barely conscious that the name had passed his lips. It might have been a thought that echoed in his mind, for all he knew. A sudden chill passed down his spine, and Souders knew he had to see his daughter, speak to her at once. Transmit a warning if he could.

If it wasn't too late.

Where was she? School, this time of day. He didn't know her schedule, but there must be some way to find out in case of emergency. The records office, for example. He could call them up and—

No.

He drove on past his neighborhood and kept on going, bound for San Francisco State. If he was wrong, his fears unfounded, then the worst she'd suffer was a moment of embarrassment. When both of them were safe and sound, beyond a shadow of a doubt, they could sit down together, have a drink and laugh it off.

But not today.

He wouldn't run the risk with Corey's life.

Accelerating in defiance of the posted limit, almost hoping for a black-and-white to show up in his mirror, Vernon Souders hurried on his way.

And prayed he wasn't too late.

THE ONLY PAVED ROAD entering Balboa Park was christened for a local military hero, Sergeant John V. Young. For all his years of living in the city, Barney Gibson couldn't say what Sergeant Young had done, or where he did it, but he wished the soldier well.

This afternoon he wished *all* soldiers well.

He didn't look for Bolan, going in. They hadn't specified a meeting place inside the park, but he'd make it obvious. He left his cruiser in the public parking lot and started walking back in the direction of concession stands. Along the way he made a game of checking faces, watching shadows from the corner of his eye, imagining how Bolan would approach this time when it was his turn.

He was painting mustard on a foot-long hot dog when the too-familiar voice advised him, "Those things take five years off your life."

"I'm not that lucky," Gibson told him, chomping on the dog before he turned. "The way it works with me, I'll wind up with the one that makes you live forever, so I never get to pull the pin."

"That bad?"

"Some days. Most times it's worse. You having anything?"

"Just coffee," Bolan replied, toasting him with a foam cup.

"Now there's a health brew for you."

"Right."

"Let's stroll."

When they were out of earshot from the food stands, Gibson said, "I think you're coming up on trouble."

"What else is new?"

"Guy down at GIU told me about this snitch he's got inside the gangs."

"Nice work if you can get it."

"All the perks, you bet. One slip, they cut your gonads off and nail them to your mama's door."

"About that snitch..."

"He says the Skulls and Nomads had a sit-down just this morning and supposedly they're closing ranks. You won't guess why."

"I might at that."

"Do give."

"Your version first."

"Okay. Somebody spread the word that a honkie dude's been pulling down a number of the bigger hits in town—divide and conquer time. I don't know if the warlords are convinced or faking it, but word out on the street says they'll be laying differences aside...at least for now. Your move."

"During the gig on Fisher Avenue, I lost my mask. You had to be there. Anyway, one of their bimbos saw me, but she wasn't armed. I didn't waste her."

"That's Skulls," Gibson said, "and I have a sneaking hunch there's more to this."

The warrior shrugged, almost indifferent to the risk he was incurring in the City by the Bay. "I picked a Nomad dealer off the street this morning and told him all about how One Shot Johnson and the Skulls were paying to me to burn the Nomads down. Thing is, they've stiffed me now and I'm a little miffed. Enough to spread the word at least."

"Hell's bells, you never miss a trick."

"I hope that's true."

"So now, the way you figure it, the Skulls go running to the Nomads with their story of a white man shooting up the Fisher Arms, but Playboy Raymond has to figure it's a scam because this white dude's working for the Skulls.''

"*Was* working for the Skulls," Bolan corrected. "If he buys the whole package, he has to figure I'm a loose canon now, short fifty large and mighty pissed off at somebody."

"So far so good. But if the Nomads came back with a challenge that this honkie gun's been working for the Skulls, we could have had ourselves a civil war right there."

"Unless the Nomads held a little something back, or else pretended they were buying it to work some angle of their own."

"Like what?"

"I wouldn't have a clue offhand. It makes it nice, though, when your enemy decides he wants to be your friend and stick real close. It always lets you know right where he is in case you want to reach out and touch someone one of these days."

"An inside job?"

"Could be. Of course, there's still one other possibility."

Before he spoke the words the captain knew he really didn't want to know. And still he asked. "What's that?"

"They rap a while and come up with a rough approximation of the truth. It's always been a risk, this kind of game. They won't know who I am, of course, or who I represent, but they'll get focused on the common enemy you talked about."

"That's all I need," the captain groused. "Some kind of goddamn supergang out hunting for the Executioner in San Francisco. Tell me something, will you? Honestly?"

"I'll try."

"You haven't got some kind of a messiah complex since the last time, have you? Maybe reading up on martyrs now and then?"

"It's not my style."

"Okay, I'm sold. Now all you have to do is sell the Skulls and Nomads while you're at it."

"Best thing for it is to let them stew a little bit."

"Low boiling point these hoods. They get pissed off or feel betrayed, they like to hit back yesterday."

"They have to find me first," the soldier said, but even as he spoke there came another thought to wipe his smile away.

"What is it?" Gibson asked.

"Let's say I need to mend some fences PDQ."

"Be careful, will you?"

"It's my middle name."

And that, Captain Barney Gibson thought, was the biggest single lie he'd heard all week.

15

"Nobody told me we were goin' back to school," a gunner in the rear compartment of the van complained.

The Z Man wasn't having any of it. "No one's expectin' you to read a book or anything," he snapped. "Now y'all shut up back there and let me think."

"You got ambition, cuz."

He spun and pinned the big mouth with a glare that would have frozen lava on a downhill slope. "Somebody ask for your opinion?"

"Naw."

"Then zip your fuckin' lip before I have to cut it off and shove it up your ass to keep your daddy company."

The Z Man half expected a response, already had the six-inch switchblade nestled in his palm, but there was nothing. Silence reigned in the back as they proceeded north on Nineteenth Avenue along the eastern boundary of San Francisco State University.

"Just take your time," he told the driver. "We've got plenty, and we know the building where she's got her class. Let's check the parkin' lot and see what we can see."

"Some kind of blue, I think it was," the driver said.

"A blue Chevette. You're right on time, my man."

The Z Man could remember stories of the old days at the school, Black Students Union and the Panthers going up against the white administration for some justice, shutting down the place until the pigs rolled through and gaffled everybody up. It didn't get as wild as Berkeley, or the riots in the Point, but Z Man thought it must have been some funky action all the same.

Today was strictly hit-and-run, no messages, no slogans painted on the walls. If everything went down the way it was supposed to, no one would remember they were even there—that is, until they made their move on the old man.

The strategy was vague in parts, where Z Man's briefing was concerned, but he was used to operating halfway in the dark. A part of him resented it at first, but later on he understood it made good sense. If he got busted somehow and the oinkers went to work on him the way they did with brothers in the lockup, there was only so much he could spill. It minimized the risk to all concerned.

And that made Z Man feel as if he was playing on a pretty special team.

The way he understood it, it was One Shot's plan to grab the bitch and trade her off some way against the old man who was making waves. The Z Man didn't understand precisely what they hoped to gain, but it wasn't important that he know. The main thing was precision execution of his orders, pulling off the snatch without mistakes.

Experience had shown him how the warlord hated it when one of his selected schemes went down the crapper due to someone else's fucking up. He never screamed and yelled about it, but he always paid the fuckup back some way, in spades.

No fuckups then at any price. And if they *did* fuck up, he meant to lay the blame on someone else.

It struck him as a fair and foolproof plan.

"That's blue," the driver told him, pointing toward a compact car immediately on their left.

"It's also a Toyota, man. I mentioned a Chevette, if you recall."

"Oh. Right."

The blue Chevette was four rows over near the end. They didn't have a license number or a photograph for confirmation, and the Z Man made a snap decision to avoid the risk of breaking in to check the registration papers in the glove compartment. There was time yet, if they used it properly.

"Remember this one," he commanded, knowing in his heart he'd have to do all the remembering himself. "We'll take another drive around and make damn sure there ain't no other blue Chevettes we missed."

"If you say so, man."

"That's what I say."

If One Shot had the timing down, they still had close to fifteen minutes, ample time to cruise the parking lot for copycats and make it back in time to bag a space nearby. And if they couldn't find a place to park, well, what the hell. They'd just keep driving, circling like a big gray shark until they found what they were looking for and grabbed her.

THE REGISTRATION OFFICE seemed to be a mile away from anything that mattered, with a tiny parking lot for visitors where every space was filled. Disgusted with the time he was wasting, Vernon Souders took a space reserved for faculty, deciding he'd rather take the parking ticket—even have the damn car towed away—than gamble with his daughter's life.

He followed signs to find the registrar, found her office and kept the story minimal, no gangs, no threats. It was a simple family crisis, and Corey was needed back at home without delay. If she would only pull the schedule card and tell him where his daughter might be found...

"Of course, you understand I'll need ID," she said.

"Excuse me?"

"We make every effort to protect our students from harassment, sir. I have no doubt you *are* a member of the family, of course, but you can see that anyone might walk in off the street and say the same. A valid driver's license will be adequate, I think."

He passed it over with a frown. "You don't think this might be a phony?"

She was on the verge of laughing when she caught his look.

"Perhaps I'd better see a credit card or two, as well."

He spilled the contents of his wallet and let her take her pick. When she was satisfied about his name and address, both recorded with painstaking slowness on a yellow legal pad, she pushed the jumble back at him and took a slow stroll to the bank of filing cabinets set behind her desk.

"The student's name again?"

"It's Corey Souders."

She sidestepped to the second cabinet in line and bent to the third drawer down. Pulling up a slim manila folder, she left it standing crooked, like a bookmark, so she wouldn't lose her place. The pink slip in her hand was five-by-seven, an apparent copy of the schedule sheet. He watched her set it to one side, returning to the file and pulling out another sheet or paper, double-checking information from the legal pad against the file.

It struck him that the woman was confirming his ID as Corey's father. Under other circumstances Souders would have been relieved to see his daughter's privacy protected by a dragon lady. At the moment, though, her sluggish movements made him want to scream.

"Well, this appears to be in order," she decided after several precious moments, straightening the file again. "You'll find her in Psychology 300. That's in Bowman Hall. The far side of the campus, I'm afraid."

She pointed toward a beige brick wall, as if his X-ray eyes could show him how to get there.

"Would you have a campus map available, by any chance?"

"Of course. Just let me think. Where *can* those be?"

Three minutes were shot to hell before she found the map and drew an *X* to indicate where they were standing, with an arrow stretching out to jab a building that looked miles away.

"Class ends at 2:15."

He checked his watch. Six minutes! Jesus Christ!

Souders left the office and seconds later was racing past groups of students idling on the quad. He felt eyes upon him as he passed, and voices called after him if he impinged too closely on their space. One coed spilled her books, and Souders shouted an apology across his shoulder as he kept on running, wondering for just a moment if her boyfriend might give chase.

It couldn't hurt at that. Maybe even pick up some campus cops along the way for backup when he got to Corey's class.

There was no reason why the animals should make their move on campus when they had all day and night, but something in the back of Souders's mind was telling him they wouldn't care to wait. If One Shot and the Skulls were pissed enough, they'd risk anything.

Approaching Bowman Hall, he slowed enough to catch his breath and check his watch. Late, goddamn it! He'd missed the change of class, but he might still catch Corey if she lingered afterward for small talk with her friends.

He made his way inside the building, swimming upstream against the press of exiting students, forced to scan each face as best he could for fear of missing Corey in the crush. But there was no sign of her before he reached the classroom that the registrar had fingered for him.

Empty.

Souders saw their next assignment written on the chalk board, then glanced around the room as if he might expect to pick up Corey's essence like a spoor for him to follow.

Nothing. He was losing precious time.

Outside, he gambled on expediency, turning toward the nearest student parking lot.

If only there was time.

Please, God, let there be time!

WHEN COREY DROPPED her books, she thought it was symptomatic of her day in general. She had barely managed sitting through her class, and now that Corey tried, she found she couldn't recall a single major feature from the lecture.

Damn it!

Damn her father and his private war against the gangs in Hunters Point. She wondered if it was a flashback to his military days that had made him so determined to take charge and put things right. As if the neighbors even gave a damn, so anxious just to get away that they were listing houses left and right at bargain rates.

A wiser, less courageous man would let it go and get out while he had a chance before he placed his life at jeopardy a second time, perhaps without the luck that had seen him through the last time.

Scooping up her scattered books, she tucked them underneath an arm and started toward her car. The lot was full, a gray van circling for a space. The driver could have hers if he was quick enough and saw her pulling out.

She set her books on the fender, digging in her purse for keys. A moment's fumbling under lipstick, compacts, pens and tissues, then she had them in her hand. Behind her the van slowed to wait while she backed out.

No, they were closer. Almost right on top of her, it sounded like. She straightened, turning toward the sound in time to feel a rough hand clasped across her mouth. The other arm was looped around her waist, and Corey's feet thrashed air as she was lifted and carried toward the van. She lost one shoe and used the other to kick at her captor's legs.

"You better watch that, bitch!"

The hand against her face clamped tighter, twisting until Corey thought her cheeks would rip. She whimpered, tears of pain streaming down her face and across the fingers of that ruthless hand.

"Get in there now!" the stranger snapped. And to another young man in the van said, "Make sure she's quiet, understand?"

"No sweat."

Corey landed on her hands and knees, rough metal hard against her palms, and she seized the moment, twisting toward the side door of the van before it closed. Blunt fingers tangled in her hair and dragged her backward. She was trapped, but she wasn't without a voice.

"Please, help—"

The fist came out of darkness, striking her above one eye and dropping the girl to the floor. Her vision blurred, and she could find no breath with which to shout.

Still time. The door was moving on its rollers, but she still saw daylight through the gap, and students moving on the distant quad. She rolled in that direction, met another looping fist, and the explosive impact flipped her over onto her back.

The door slammed shut, but Corey never saw it. She was lost in darkness of her own.

THE PHONE RANG seven times before he got an answer. At first Bolan didn't recognize the sound of Vernon Souders's voice.

"Hello?"

"I'm checking in."

There was no recognition problem on the other end as Souders caught his breath. A slight change in the tone, but Bolan couldn't say with any certainty if what he heard was panic or relief.

"Dear God, you've got to help me!"

Bolan felt a worm of dread uncoiling in his gut.

"What is it?"

"Corey. She's been kidnapped." Souders's voice was trembling on the breaking point. "They've taken her."

"*Who*'s taken her?"

"The Skulls, I think."

"You think?"

The story came out piecemeal, starting with the morning's demonstration and the threat from One Shot Johnson, Souders's frightened race over to the university and getting there too late, his daughter's car abandoned in the student parking lot, a long drive home, not certain she was missing yet, still praying for another explanation that would wipe his fears away.

And then the phone call, mocking laughter on the line and a promise that his daughter would die slowly, screaming, if he didn't give "the white dude" up.

"What have you said to the police?"

"I didn't call them," Souders said. "They told me if I get the cops involved, it's Corey's life."

No kidnapping report meant no tap on the line. The warrior took a breath, determined not to rush.

"What kind of deadline are you on?"

"I went in playing dumb and tried to stall the best I could, but they weren't buying it. They want delivery by midnight."

"Where?"

"They didn't say. Somebody's supposed to call."

Eight hours, give or take, assuming the setup call would come at least an hour or so before the meet. A lot could happen in that length of time.

"Okay, you're staying by the telephone, correct? Don't leave the house for any reason."

"No, I won't."

"I might send someone by to see you in a little while. If so, it's safe for you to trust him. Tell him everything."

"They said—"

"I know what you were told," he interrupted Souders, hating what he had to say and how it made him feel. "And you know they can't afford to let her live. The chances are she's safe right now because they know you might demand some proof before you make the drop. Once you deliver, it's a wrap. They have to kill you both. No witnesses, no case."

"I understand."

The tone of Souders's voice told Bolan he'd reached the same conclusions on his own.

"All right. No matter what you hear from this point on, you have to realize I'm doing everything I can to get your daughter back, alive and well."

"What are you—"

"I'm not sure exactly." That much was the truth, although he had a fair idea. "Before we have a chance to deal I have to get their full attention."

"Mr. Blanski?"

"Yes."

"If something...happens..." Souders hesitated, running out of words and energy. It took a moment for him to collect himself. "I mean to say..."

"Don't worry," Bolan told him, taking up the slack. "Nobody skates on this one. Any way it plays, they're going down."

"I feel so helpless, sitting here. If there was only something I could do."

"You're doing it," the Executioner replied. "The other end is mine."

"Okay."

"I'll be in touch."

He cradled the receiver, thinking fast. It would be tricky, sounding Barney Gibson out and hoping he'd treat the matter with discretion. Any kind of law-enforcement turnout could be fatal at the moment, but the captain's first response would be to put the wheels in motion, playing by the book. With any luck he had a chance to get beyond that and allow himself some lead time for a move against the Skulls.

Or *was* it just the Skulls?

The threat from One Shot Johnson took his mind in that direction, but he also had to deal with the report from Gibson, that the Skulls and Nomads had secured some kind of loose alliance for the moment, closing ranks against a common enemy.

Himself.

Assuming that was true, he had to treat both gangs as equal partners in the move on Corey Souders. And he had to take whatever steps he could to get her back at any cost.

It was a game the Executioner had played before, but it was never easy. Gambling with another's life, especially when that person was a total innocent, took every ounce of nerve and dedication he could muster. If he blew it, Corey Souders would be dead, her father would be devastated and the blood would be on Bolan's hands.

But if he took no action, merely sat it out, the end result would be the same.

No choice at all.

One call to make before he hit the streets again, and there was precious little time to waste.

The Executioner had places to go and people to kill.

16

The room was small, no more than ten feet square in Corey Souders's estimation. It was also windowless, the only door directly opposite from where Corey huddled on the floor. Her wrists were cuffed behind her back, but they'd left her ankles free, as if she had somewhere to go.

Her prison cell was stuffy from a lack of circulation, but there was no heating, and a chill crept in despite the fact that it was warm outside. A part of that, she knew, was coming from inside herself, a physical reaction to the fact of being kidnapped and detained by people whom she knew wouldn't mind killing her if they believed it necessary.

On the other hand, they might decide to kill her just for fun.

She didn't recognize her captors, but she knew enough about the local gangs to realize that wearing blue plaid flannel shirts meant they were members of the Skulls. From there it was an easy step to understanding that she'd be used against her father somehow, but she wouldn't chase the thought beyond that point.

It panicked her to think of death, and Corey knew she'd need her mind in perfect working order if she meant to walk away from this experience. Her father would be doing everything he could to help her, but she had a reasonable understanding of the risks involved for both of them.

Her captors hadn't taken any pains to hide their faces, and she knew that was bad. If they weren't afraid of witnesses, it meant they weren't expecting any to survive. She was alive because they needed her that way—perhaps to keep the pressure on her father. They could easily have killed her in the parking lot and made their getaway, but they'd brought her to this cell instead.

Some kind of bargain then. Or, rather, the suggestion of a deal, proposed to trick her father, force his hand somehow or make him offer an exchange. Himself for Corey?

Two dead on the pavement when he kept the date.

It crossed her mind that there was still a way to cheat the bastards if they needed her alive and well. If she could find a way...

But, no.

It went against her nature, thinking suicide, and she'd have no chance to pull it off in any case. The room was bare of furniture, likewise potential weapons, and with Corey's hands cuffed tightly behind her there was little she could do to harm herself if she was so inclined. It was impossible to hold your breath until you died, and if she slammed her head against the wall repeatedly, the maximum result would be unconsciousness, with one horrendous headache when she came around.

So much for sacrifice.

Escaping from her cell didn't appear to be an option. She'd tried the door and found it locked. She could resist and try to break away when they came back for her, but she wasn't encouraged by the prospect of attacking one or more armed Skulls with nothing but her teeth and feet.

Unconscious when they brought her to this room, she had no way of telling where she was or how much time had passed. The crust of blood above one eye had dried, but Corey had no training that would let her estimate how long it took a scab to form. She'd been conscious for at least an hour, and the rumbling in her stomach told her she was hungry, but the rest was merely guesswork.

Corey wondered if the police were looking for her, or perhaps the federal agent known as Blanski. In the movies ransom notes inevitably carried warnings not to call the law, and she assumed the Skulls were bright enough to tack on similar provisions of their own. She wondered if her father would comply with such instructions, thinking of the times when he'd been ignored or put on hold by the police, or whether he'd take the chance of calling in official help.

She had no personal experience with kidnapping; the media had been her teacher, and it bothered Corey that she hadn't paid enough attention when she had the choice. There should be *something* she could do, if only—

Wait.

It was traditional, she understood, for parties facing ransom threats to ask for proof that hostages were still alive before they finally agreed to various demands. The action made for tearful or suspenseful scenes, depending on the way it played, but in real life it meant a last chance to communicate before her father stepped into the trap.

She had a chance to save his life, if not her own. But first—

Her thoughts were interrupted by the sound of foot-steps on the far side of the door, keys jingling as the lock was turned. One of the Skulls entered the room, two others visible behind him, blocking access to a dingy, narrow hall. The new arrival dropped a greasy bag in front of her, and Corey's nostrils flared as she smelled food.

"I'm takin' off the cuffs," he told her, crouching at her side and leaning close enough for her to smell his rancid breath. "Be good and eat your supper now, keep up your strength. You might need it by and by."

He spent a moment fondling her breasts, the others watching from the hallway, grinning as they nudged each other, and she bit her tongue to keep from cursing them. With no response he gave it up and reached behind her, twisting Corey's arms at awkward angles while he fumbled with the cuffs.

"Be back to see you later, bitch," he told her, rising and retreating toward the door. "Don't go away."

The door swung shut, and Corey heard the lock engage before she brought her hands around in front of her and flexed her fingers, bringing back the circulation in a painful rush.

Inside the bag she found a smallish burger and some onion rings. Instead of bolting it, she took her time and made it last. It was a poor last meal, but it was all she had.

And he was right about conserving energy, oh, yes.

She had her hands back now, and everything had changed.

A fighting chance perhaps. If she failed...well, dead was dead, and Corey Souders knew she had very little left to lose.

"SHE COOL?"

Weed grinned and licked his lips. "I'd say she hot."

"Forget about that shit," the warlord of the Skulls replied. "This ain't no fuckin' game."

"Who says we can't be havin' fun before we take the old man off?"

"I'm tellin' you to keep it clean until we make the touch. He's going to want his baby safe and sound before he makes delivery."

Weed's grin had done a turnaround, the corners of his mouth surrendering to gravity.

"Okay, cuz. No big thing."

"We wrap this up, y'all have plenty time to celebrate in style. Get lost and let me think a while."

Alone again the warlord of the Skulls reflected on how easy it had been, so far.

Too easy?

He'd gone into the meet with Playboy Raymond and the Nomads half expecting bloodshed, certain he'd have to sell his story of the white dude using everything he had. Instead it felt as if Playboy had come in *wanting* to believe him, laying out a story of his own about Candy Man and how this honkie had tried to put the whole thing on the Skulls.

Some kind of crazy shit, but One Shot figured there was more to what was going down than met the eye. Someone else was involved, and once you ruled out the Sicilians that left old man Souders and his coffee club. From there it was an easy step to lining up the snatch and putting pressure on until the fucker bent.

It was the kind of game Johnson understood. A classic squeeze, with no place for the mark to run, and when you had him in your hand, you kept the pressure on until there wasn't any opposition left. The only rivals One Shot Johnson trusted were the dead kind, and he liked to pull the trigger himself. Less chance of a mistake that way, and it cut down on overhead.

He had no doubt Souders would attempt to meet their terms, but Johnson wondered if the problem could be solved that easily. The story Playboy Raymond told was something else again. If it was true that Souders had employed a mercenary and decided not to pay him off on time, the old man's chances of delivering the honkie on demand were nil. Assuming he could reach the man at all, he was as likely to get wasted for his trouble as to sell another pitch and bring the shooter back in line.

It wouldn't bother Johnson in the least if someone else should bust the cap on Souders, but he didn't like to think about the shooter hanging out, already pissed and thinking up new ways to take it out against the Skulls.

Ideally he'd like to bring the white dude in alive and have a chance to question him before they put him down. There was a fifty-fifty chance that he was working with accomplices, and Johnson meant to clear the slate before he let the matter rest.

Loose ends could get a brother killed, and no mistake.

He checked the stolen Rolex watch on his wrist. They still had seven hours left before the meet, say six before he had Weed call the old man back with the directions. Nothing fancy, but a place he'd agreed on with the No-mads, where a welcoming committee would be waiting to receive their enemies.

And afterward . . . then, what?

He trusted Playboy Raymond no more than he had before the shooting started, no more than he trusted

Vernon Souders now. When they finished with the job at hand, there would be no good reason to maintain the unaccustomed truce.

But this time, when the shooting started, One Shot Johnson didn't plan to waste his time on penny-ante drive-bys, picking off the Numbnuts one punk at a time.

You want to wipe out a nest of roaches, the best way was to get them all together, hit the frigging nest with everything you had and watch them fry. It might not be within his reach to waste the Savage Nomads root and branch, but he could do the next best thing.

Playboy's time was running out. Dumb bastard didn't know it yet, but he was walking toward an open grave.

And One Shot Johnson was about to help him take the fall.

VERNON SOUDERS ANSWERED the doorbell with a Colt .45 automatic in his hand and a grim expression on his face. The look stayed with him when he recognized Barney Gibson, but at least he eased down the pistol's hammer.

"I hope that's registered," Gibson said.

"Some of us obey the law, for what it's worth."

"May I come in?"

"I answered all your questions last time, Captain."

"Something new's come up."

"Such as?"

"Your daughter's been abducted, I believe."

The black man's shoulders sagged. "Oh, God."

"I'd really rather not discuss this on the porch."

"All right."

Reluctantly Souders unlatched the screen and stood aside as Gibson entered the house. When he latched the screen again and double-locked the door, he joined the captain in the living room. "He said there might be someone coming by."

A frown from Gibson. "He?"

"I think we understand each other, Captain. Please sit down."

"The first thing you should understand is that I represent the San Francisco Police Department. No one else."

"Of course."

"Our policy on kidnapping is strictly by the book. We place the victim's safety first, and do our best to expedite the family's wishes in regard to any ransom payments while employing every means available to capture the abductors. For the record, we don't advise cooperation with demands. The record frankly doesn't indicate a high rate of success where ransom is involved."

"I couldn't meet their price, regardless," Souders said. "It isn't money they want."

"I understand." The captain's tone was solemn. "I believe you'll find they get exactly what they're asking for."

"But how...?"

"I don't have any details, and I wouldn't be at liberty to share them if I did. Let's say I've been around this block before, and let it go at that."

"But Mr. Blanski..."

"Is an expert at the kind of thing he does. It wouldn't be the first time he's retrieved a hostage, but you have to understand the risks involved."

"I think I have a fair idea." A touch of bitter irony showed in Souders's voice.

"I hope so," Gibson said. "First thing, you need to realize that scrubbing witnesses is SOP among the kind of folks we're dealing with. They don't like going into court if they can help it, and there's no way they intend to let your daughter live. You, either."

"I've considered the alternatives."

"Okay. With that in mind the best thing you can do to help yourself is cop a fatalistic attitude. I don't mean giving up, by any means, but it would be a flat-out lie to tell you the odds were on your side."

"You sound like a lieutenant I once knew."

"Would that be Vietnam?"

"It's ancient history. I've got another war to fight just now."

"Correction. Someone else is carrying the ball on this play. Anything you do would only slow him down and further jeopardize your daughter's life."

"So I've been told. They also serve who only man the phone."

"It happens to be true. When these pricks call back, do you want to miss it? Maybe start them thinking they should scrub the deal and try another angle of attack?"

"I'm here," Souders replied. "What else can I do?"

"For now that's it. It might be helpful if I put a tracer on your line, perhaps an officer inside the house."

"No guards," the black man told him flatly. "It's a risk just talking to you even now. For all I know they could be watching, taking note of who stops by."

"If anybody asks, just tell them I came by to chew you out about this morning's demonstration. Now about that tracer—"

"What's the point? I understand they always use a pay phone in a case like this."

"Not necessarily. It doesn't take a genius to abduct a woman, Mr. Souders. And the address of a pay phone could be helpful in itself to narrow down a target neighborhood."

"What difference does it make? I don't want the police involved. These bastards see a SWAT team coming and my daughter's as good as dead."

"Did someone mention the police?"

"You said—"

"I said the information could be useful to a rescue. Frankly I don't see why SWAT should have to be involved."

"It seems to me you're gambling with your career."

"We never had this conversation," Gibson said. "Officially I'm on the other side of town right now, investigating leads on one of last night's homicides. I wouldn't be surprised if there were witnesses to that effect."

"I see."

"My point is, Mr. Souders, that the best man for the job is already working on it."

"I wonder, Captain . . . who exactly *is* this man?"

"A specialist. That's really all that I can say."

"Are your superiors aware of his activities?"

"I think I've overstayed my welcome," Gibson said. "About that tracer . . ."

"Yes, all right."

"I'll send a man who fits the neighborhood. He won't be driving a department car."

"I'll be here," Souders said. "There's nowhere else for me to go."

He let the captain out, made sure the doors were locked again and walked back to the living room with leaden strides. The house felt empty—no, abandoned—as he sat down in his chair beside the telephone and placed the heavy automatic pistol in his lap.

Grim silence kept him company as he resumed the wait.

THE TRICK, BOLAN THOUGHT, would be letting someone live to take the message back. A simple in-and-out required the minimal finesse, avoiding stray civilian casualties while dropping every enemy in sight. The task of sparing one or two when they were actively involved in fighting back was rather more involved.

He chose the Nomad hangout for a start because he still believed both gangs were linked somehow to the abduction. If his judgment was in error, it would do no harm to keep the pressure on and let the Nomads know they were suffering for what the Skulls had done.

From what the Executioner could see the only innocents involved were Corcy Souders and her father, with the others who had made their stand against the local gangs.

The clubhouse was an outpost of the Nomad turf on Tisdale Drive. He left his car in an alley two doors down and went in through the back, a six-foot wooden fence no real impediment at all. The warrior wore his black-suit, but his face and hands were bare. The silenced Uzi slapped against Bolan's hip as he jogged across the yard and cleared a wedge of patio to reach the sliding doors.

No point in standing on formalities, he thought, and hit the broad glass sliders with a burst that brought them down in jagged, crashing sheets. Inside he caught two Nomads lurching off the couch and nailed them with Parabellum manglers, dumping them together in a heap.

Another charged in to join the action, coming from a kitchen on the left. The soldier spun to face his adversary, laying down a knee-high burst that cut the runner's legs from under him, and dropped him squirming onto the threadbare carpet. Stepping in to close the gap, he kicked the Nomad's .38 away and cracked the Uzi's folding stock against his skull.

Lights out, and Bolan had his messenger wrapped up.

The rest could go.

He caught three Nomads creeping down the hall, reluctant to approach the sounds of battle, stuck with no way out unless they saw it through. All three were packing, and they opened up as Bolan stuck his head around the corner, spraying plaster dust in all directions, missing the warrior by a yard.

He palmed a frag grenade and armed it, crouching as he made the pitch. There was another burst of hasty fire, and then he heard the Nomads shouting, cursing, tripping over one another as they tried to get away.

Too late.

The blast brought down a portion of the flimsy ceiling, powdering their bodies with a rain of plaster dust. One of them stirred slightly as the Executioner passed by, and Bolan left him there, his future in the hands of fate.

The three remaining rooms were dark and empty, silence filling in the spaces where the sounds of combat had withdrawn. He backtracked to the littered living room and brought the sure survivor back around by twisting on his ears until the pain cut through his mental fog.

"Hey, shit!"

He received more pain when he attempted to do something with his legs and found he couldn't.

"Aw, Jesus!"

"Listen up," the Executioner commanded, leveling the silencer beneath the young man's nose. "You hear me?"

"Yeah. Don't kill me, shit, man, please."

"Survival has a price. Can you remember something?"

"Huh? Sure, Jesus, yeah."

"Tell Playboy Raymond that the white dude wants the girl, unharmed. Can you remember that?"

"White dude. Don't hurt a girl."

"*The* girl."

"The girl. I got it, man."

"So live."

He put that house of death behind him, moving on. One down, and Bolan had a list of stops to make before he satisfied himself that he'd done his best for Corey Souders. When the word had time to filter back, then it would be a different game.

Or not.

He couldn't guarantee how her abductors would react, but he could promise one thing.

If she was killed or harmed in any way, there would be no place in the city for a member of the gangs to hide. The world wouldn't be big enough.

The Executioner was blitzing on.

17

He recognized Weed's footsteps coming back, and One Shot Johnson cringed inside. The feeling made him angry, touching off a throbbing ache behind one eye. It had to be bad news, and he was sick to death of watching all his plans disintegrate.

"What now?" he asked his number two, not really wanting a response.

"Another hit," Weed replied. "Four Nomads parked outside a store on Robinson. One still alive. Same message from the man."

He didn't have to ask about the content or the phrasing of the message. It had been the same each time.

The white dude wants the girl.

This thing was getting out of hand, and he'd nearly phoned a hasty threat to Vernon Souders when he caught himself. It could be what the bastards wanted, pushing him to make a dumb mistake like calling on his own line while they ran some kind of instant trace. He wasn't up on the technology, but Johnson knew there were machines that printed out your number when the other phone began to ring before the party you were calling even picked it up. Forget about the old days when it took five minutes or whatever to complete a trace.

No thanks.

Besides, a threat to Souders might not carry any weight. Suppose the old man had been messing with his shooter and had lost control somehow. The guy was out there acting like a wild man now, and it was like a fifty-fifty chance Souders couldn't stop him if wanted to. In that case, if they went ahead and iced the girl, or even took the old man down, their enemy would still be out there, kicking ass.

The only problem with the wild-card theory was his asking for the girl to be released, unharmed. If he was down on Souders, why the hell should Mr. Honkie give a shit what happened to the bitch?

Unless perhaps he wanted her to use on Souders for himself.

A little extra leverage maybe when he made another call to ask for what was owed him for his raids against the gangs.

That much made sense to Johnson's mind, but it didn't encourage hope. If he was right in his suspicion, then it meant Souders couldn't bring the shooter anywhere upon demand, and they were wasting time—along with all the homeboys who were getting dusted in the bargain. If the shooter was a wild card, he'd have to try another angle of attack . . . but what?

He didn't even know the honkie's name, for Christ's sake. How was he supposed to get in touch and make a deal, assuming he wanted to?

"How many is that now?"

"Let's see . . ." Weed stood there, frowning, counting on his fingers like a child. "Four hits so far, nine Skulls and seven Nomads dead."

"He wants the fuckin' girl so bad, he ought to leave his number," Johnson muttered, playing with his six-inch switchblade nervously.

"Could be he doesn't want the bitch at all," Weed said.

"So why's he leavin' men alive at every hit to bring the same damn message back? You want to tell me that, if you got it figured out?"

"Could be he's turnin' up the heat. Dude knows that if he hits the Nomads same as us, they come around and tell us we should lose the bitch."

"What difference does it make if he doesn't want her, anyway?"

"The difference is, it keeps us fightin' with the Nomads, killin' one another off and savin' him some trouble."

"Playboy says he's off the job already."

"Maybe so, and maybe not. Don't matter much if he's a contract hitter like they say. He won't be leavin' town until he gets his bread from somewhere, and it all spends out the same."

"So, like, you think he's wanting us to pay him off?"

"Whoever, cuz. I'm tellin' you, a guy like this doesn't give a shit. The money's green, regardless."

Johnson thought about it, frowning to himself. "Why doesn't he give us some way we can get in touch?"

"He'll get in touch with us, I wouldn't be surprised. First thing, he has to kick some ass and make sure everybody knows how bad he is."

"I get the picture," Johnson said.

"Thing is, the dude likes his work."

A thought was forming in the back of Johnson's mind, a way of settling his problem when the call came through. It wouldn't be the softest job he'd ever pulled, but it could work.

Provided the shooter gave him half a chance.

"Okay," he said at last. "We'll just be cool and wait."

"How long?" Weed asked.

"Until I tell you different, cuz."

THE VIDEO ARCADE on Kirkwood was an independent operation theoretically, but the proprietor had found it "wise" to let the Skulls move in and use his storeroom as a kind of home away from home. Most nights a group of six or seven could be found inside the back room of the Power House, conducting business and exchanging stories of their prowess on the streets while several dozen games kept up a nonstop racket in the main arcade.

The storeroom had a separate entrance, granting access to an alleyway in back, and Bolan chose that route in lieu of kicking off a firefight in the arcade proper where civilian casualties were guaranteed. The solitary guard outside was smoking like a chimney, pacing back and forth until he saw the Executioner approaching from the west, a faceless silhouette with streetlights at his back.

He wouldn't draw and fire immediately, Bolan thought. Despite his nerves the lookout was conditioned to expect foot traffic in the alley, everything from working men returning home to prostitutes escorting tricks to someplace nice and private for a little one-on-one.

The momentary hesitation was his edge.

He had the silenced 93-R in his hand as he approached the rear of the arcade. In another moment the sentry would see his face and realize he wasn't black. From that point on it could go either way.

A head shot, closing in from twenty feet, and there was never any question of a miss. One Parabellum crusher closed the gap and slammed his human target back against the cinder blocks, a dazed expression on his face. The dead man slithered down the wall into a seated posture, curling over on his side from there, all done without a sound.

Okay, so far.

A gentle touch confirmed the door was locked, and Bolan weighed his choices. It was made of steel and opened outward, two strikes against a sudden entry that would take the others by surprise. That left a sucker play, and Bolan thought he was equal to the task.

He knocked three times and muttered something incoherent in his best impression of a ghetto accent, hoping there had been no coded knock or prearranged password. A moment passed before he was rewarded by the turning of the doorknob and a shaft of light that fell across his shoes.

"Say what?"

He jerked the door wide open, and the chunky Skull was thrown off balance, pitching forward when a bullet in the forehead saved him from a nasty fall. The Executioner brushed past him even as he toppled backward to the floor.

Inside the room four others gaped at him, stunned by grim death suddenly appearing in their midst. The skinny gangster on his left recovered first, a hand thrust underneath his jacket in search of iron, and Bolan shot him twice before he had a chance to draw.

The sleek Beretta kept on tracking, satisfied to put a mangler through the next punk's shoulder, spinning him around and slamming him face first against the nearest wall. He crumpled in a heap as Bolan swung to face the survivors, catching one about to reach an Ingram resting on a metal filing cabinet close at hand.

The Beretta chugged twice, and crimson spouted from between the gunner's shoulder blades. His forehead struck the filing cabinet with sufficient force to spring the top drawer open, catching him beneath the chin and stopping him from sliding to the floor.

One left, and Bolan shot him twice in rapid fire before the Skull could cock and fire his shiny .45. The impact of a Parabellum double-punch propelled him backward, rubber legs entangled in a folding chair that took him down. His body shuddered once before the final breath of life escaped his lips.

He crossed the storeroom, rolled the wounded gangster over onto his back and shook him until the eyes swam into focus.

"Listen up if you want to live."

"I hear you, man."

"The only reason you're still breathing is to pass a message on. The white dude wants the girl. You got that?"

"White dude wants the girl. Don't kill me, please."

"Once more."

"The white dude wants the girl, okay?"

"Okay."

THE FLASHING COLORED lights from squad cars and an ambulance produced an almost festive atmosphere around the shooting scene. The auto shop on Horne was Barney Gibson's fourth stop of the night, and he was sick of staring at bodies stretched out on the ground.

How many dead since sundown? He was losing count, but Bolan had been working overtime to whittle down the Skulls and Savage Nomads. There had been no contact with the Executioner since the beginning of his blitz, and Gibson almost wished the pager on his belt would summon him to take a call from the familiar voice.

No word on Corey Souders yet, and nothing at her father's end since they'd placed the tracer on his line. It could be that the Executioner had shocked his adversaries into thinking twice about their plan, or else they were lying low and plotting out another angle of attack. It went against all odds that they could take this kind of pounding and refrain from striking back somewhere, somehow.

Earl Weathers straightened up from checking out the nearest body, moving back to Gibson's side. "If they keep this up," he said, "Gang Intervention might be out of business in a few more days."

"Don't count your chickens, Earl. There's still a lot more waiting in the wings where these came from."

"The papers talk to you?"

"They tried. I'm keeping on the move, for what it's worth."

"They nailed me coming over," Weathers said. "Same stupid questions that you always hear. 'How soon do the police expect solutions in the latest case?' Can you believe that shit?"

"I wish we had that kind of crystal ball sometimes."

"Who doesn't? Jesus, after all the crimes they've covered, seems like one or two of them would realize you can't predict a bust like it was Thursday's weather forecast."

"One-upmanship," the captain said. "They listen to a briefing, read the handouts and they come up short on things to ask."

"I guess. Your people coming up with anything?"

"Don't ask me how soon I expect arrests, okay?"

"You got a deal."

"It's funny, though."

"What's that?"

"Each hit since nightfall," Weathers said, "we find one guy alive. It's almost like somebody planned it that way, huh?"

Too close for comfort, Gibson thought. And he said, "Coincidence. Nobody bats a thousand all the time."

"I guess. It's funny, though. The way a few of these went down, the shooters could have taken time and done it right."

"When they get pissed off, it makes them careless," Gibson offered. "Count your blessings if it gives you witnesses to work with."

"Witnesses, my ass. These whipdicks wouldn't let me have the time of day if I was helping them to set a time bomb under city hall."

"You might get lucky this time."

"Right. And if we run a little short on transportation, I can take the next bunch downtown in my UFO."

The captain forced a chuckle he didn't feel and kept his fingers crossed that Weathers wouldn't start to chase the pattern he was seeing in the series of attacks. He knew Bolan needed messengers to spread the word if he had any hope of getting Corey Souders back alive, but it could blow up in his face if he made one false move.

But how long would it take for word to filter back, with the survivors injured and surrounded by police? By now the first of them had probably been able to consult with their attorneys, friends or relatives. Whatever channel it required, the message would be passed around until it reached the animals in charge of their respective gangs.

He thought of One Shot Johnson and Playboy Raymond, sitting out the night while casualty reports piled up and Bolan's word kept coming back, immutable and inescapable.

But how would they react?

Experience had taught him that the gangs were damn near unpredictable in any circumstances, and the current pressure must be edging both the Skulls and Nomads toward the detonation point.

He checked the pager on his belt again, made certain it was working.

And he wondered who'd be around to put the pieces back together when it blew.

THE OLD GARAGE on Mahan was a chop shop owned and operated by the Savage Nomads. Auto theft wasn't the gang's chief source of cash, but it was always striving to diversify. A burglary from time to time, gunrunning, prostitution—if it brought in ready cash without the sweat and strain of honest labor, there were members of the gangs who'd give damn near anything a shot.

Most weeks, according to his brief from Barney Gibson, Playboy and the Nomads could expect their shop on Mahan to produce some ten or fifteen cars with paint and numbers altered, sometimes chopped up with torches for the parts. The vehicles that stayed intact were peddled out of town or out of state to customers who asked no questions past the bottom line.

Because the operation was illicit and the street gangs weren't big on paying off police to look the other way, the chop shop did its major business after nightfall, with the broad garage doors tightly closed, the windows painted black inside. A sentry watched the street and loitered near a button that would sound alarms inside at the approach of anything resembling danger, giving members of the crew a chance to flee through different exits and escape.

The sentry first then.

Bolan crept up on his blind side, dressed in black from head to foot, his face and hands painted in combat cosmetics, to avoid the glare of moonlight. Nearby streetlamps had been blacked out months or years ago, and no one ever got around to fixing them. The silenced Uzi tucked beneath his arm was primed and ready, with the safety off.

He'd closed within ten paces of the sentry when he saw his chance. A whistle, barely audible across the gap, and Bolan saw the hood begin to turn, still curious, not reaching for his weapon yet.

The Uzi spit a 3-round burst that ripped across the Nomad's knees and dropped him onto his face. Another second and he'd have found the strength to scream, but Bolan cracked him hard behind one ear and put him under, taking time to pull the automatic from his belt and toss it out of sight. A plastic tie secured the gunner's wrists behind him, just in case he came around before they had a chance to talk.

The rest was gravy, Bolan circling around in back to find an exit that could also serve as an entrance. It was never locked or otherwise obstructed while the crew was on the premises, and the warrior entered in a rush, the Uzi leading, cold eyes narrowing against the sudden blaze of light.

Two cars—a BMW and a new Corvette—were in the process of transfiguration, half a dozen Nomad craftsmen working at their different tasks. One of them saw death coming, but the paint gun in his hand was short on stopping power, and he settled for a warning shout before he broke and ran.

The Uzi stuttered, caught him in midstride and took him down amid a cloud of crimson paint.

He held the Uzi's trigger down and let it rip, the extra weight of the suppressor helping out with recoil as he swept the room from right to left and back again. The Beamer and the 'Vette would need more bodywork before they hit the streets again, but they were points ahead. The Nomad workmen weren't going anywhere until they made the trip downtown in rubber bags.

A couple of them almost made it, lunging for another exit hatch in lieu of standing fast and putting up a fight, but Bolan's thin edge of surprise was edge enough. The Uzi did its job efficiently, and when the smoke began to lift, his targets were unmoving on the floor. In time their blood would mingle with the paint and oil, a little something for the people at forensics to untangle when they had the time.

Outside, he breathed the relatively clean night air and fed the Uzi a brand-new magazine before he walked back to the wounded lookout. Pain had brought the guy around, and he was working on his bonds but making little progress.

The punk saw Bolan coming, and he must have figured his time was up. He stiffened, gave up tugging on the bonds that held wrists behind his back and waited for the killing blow to fall.

Instead, the warrior knelt beside him, leaning close so that the Uzi's muzzle nudged against the Nomad's chest. "You hear okay?"

"I hear you, man." The words came out through teeth clenched tight against his pain.

"I've got a message for Playboy," Bolan said. "It's worth your life to me if you can pass it on."

"That's it?"

"That's it."

"So lay it on me, man."

"The white dude wants the girl. Repeat."

He gave it back, once interrupted by a grimace, but he got it right.

"Okay?"

"Suits me," the warrior said, and left him there for the police and paramedics who would soon be closing on the scene. To make sure the action wasn't overlooked, he meant to make the call himself.

And soon it would be time for yet another kind of call.

The message had been planted, given ample time and opportunities to spread. The time was coming up for him to check and see how it had been received.

A precious life was hanging in the balance, and he felt that weight upon his shoulders as he jogged back toward the car.

Soon now. No matter how it played, the end was coming soon.

So be it.

18

The cheap wine wasn't helping him relax, and One Shot Johnson thought he might have to try some pills to bring him down if this kept up. Three hours, and he had another fifteen homeboys dead, with four recovering from lucky wounds that left them breathing. After they passed their message on—the same one every time—he almost wished they'd died, as well.

The white dude wants the girl.

Admitting a mistake didn't come easy for the warlord of the Skulls. In damn near any situation he could think of, his subordinates would never dare suggest he'd made an error, much less rub it in his face and make him squirm this way. The leader of a righteous street gang made the rules up as he went along, and anyone who disagreed could risk a challenge, if they had the strength and nerve to back it up. In practice it was seldom done unless the warlord fucked things up so bad the gang began to suffer from his personal mistakes.

Like now.

It was a brainstorm, picking up the girl and using her to pressure old man Souders, have him bring the shooter in and nail them both to make it stick. The Savage Nomads had agreed to play along by laying off until the touch was made, contributing a hit team when the time came down to finish off their common enemy. It seemed to be a perfect plan at first.

No matter how you sliced it, though, the game was blowing up in Johnson's face. It wouldn't take a genius in the ranks to calculate the growing list of dead and wounded soldiers, tracing their destruction back to One Shot's faulty judgment call.

And if it came down to a challenge, how would he defend himself? The cease-fire with the Nomads worked against him when you thought about it, making Johnson look as if he'd kissed up to the enemy and let the Numbnuts tell him what to do. If anyone was really thinking out there, it could even look as if Playboy Raymond had set up the whole thing to put the Skulls at risk.

Of course, the Nomads had been taking hits during the past few hours, as well. If nothing else, their losses blew away the argument that Playboy Raymond had devised the plan to serve himself. Unfortunately it presented Johnson with another problem he'd have to solve if he was going to survive.

He hadn't been in touch with Playboy Raymond in the past few hours, but he could imagine how the warlord of the Nomads felt, just sitting there and watching as his men got blown away. Would he suspect the Skulls of pulling off some kind of double cross despite the temporary pact the gangs had formed? Whatever else he thought about Playboy, Johnson never took him for an idiot. It must be obvious both gangs were being pounded by the enemy, but Playboy Raymond might resent the fact that Johnson's people had the girl, while raids continued on the Nomads all the same.

Was it enough to blow the truce and launch another round of hit-and-runs between the gangs? Would Playboy—

"Telephone."

The warlord swiveled in his chair and found Weed staring at him with a strange expression on his face. Bad news again, for Christ's sake. He was half-afraid to ask.

"What now?"

"The dude."

"Say what?"

Weed shrugged. "Man says to tell you he's the white dude, and it's time to settle up. Could be some kind of bullshit, for all I know."

"You think he got our number from the Yellow Pages?"

"Hey, man—"

Brushing past his number two, the warlord made his way along a narrow corridor to reach the far end of the clubhouse where they kept the building's only working telephone. He lifted the receiver gingerly, almost as if he thought it might explode.

"Who's this?"

A deep voice, calm and cold. "I hear you've been looking for me, Elroy."

"Won't know that until you tell me who it is."

"Let's cut the crap, okay?" the caller said, his voice as cold as polished steel. "You want a crack at me, I want the girl. Let's work it out."

"What put you on us, man?"

"Let's say I don't like scum, and let it go at that."

"Big talk for someone on the phone."

"If you want it face-to-face, shut up and grab a pencil. This is what you do. . . ."

"I set the meeting, man. You don't come on here tellin' me—"

"If you want to argue, Elroy, I can hang up now and kick your ass all night. All day tomorrow. All week long. How many soldiers left before you have to call up the peewees?"

A sudden throbbing headache made the warlord close his eyes. "Let's hear it then."

"You get that pencil?"

"I'll remember. Don't you worry."

"Do you know the Central Basin?"

"I can find it."

"Agua Vista Park at 1:00 a.m. Don't bother showing up without the girl."

"What else?"

"That's it."

The warlord frowned. "No shit about how I'm supposed to come alone?"

"Bring anyone you want," the caller said, and you could almost see him grinning on the other end. "The more the merrier."

The dial tone buzzed, and One Shot dropped the handset into its cradle, taking time to wipe his sweaty palm against his khaki pants. He felt Weed staring at him as he checked his watch. Three hours remained before the meet.

"Get twenty men together," he commanded. "I want automatic shit for everybody, hear me? Ready on the spot by twelve o'clock."

"Okay."

His turn to make a call, and Johnson wasn't looking forward to the exercise. Still, he couldn't avoid it. Playboy Raymond had a piece of what was going down, and it was time to share. With any luck at all the warlord of the Savage Nomads might insist on dropping by with several of his boys to watch the meet go down.

Bring anyone you want. The more the merrier.

Damn right.

And once he had his enemies together, all of them collected at a single place, it would be Johnson's turn to call the tune.

He could already hear the music in his mind.

It sounded like a funeral march.

IT TOOK A WHILE for Bolan to connect with Barney Gibson, going through his pager, but he didn't mind. Three hours, give or take, before the final act went down, and there was ample time for him to make his preparations at the scene.

He'd deliberately insisted on a piece of neutral ground away from Hunters Point where Skulls and Nomads would be off their native turf. It made retreat more difficult for troops accustomed to the confines of their neighborhood, and the topography would let him have some combat stretch. As for civilians, he was counting on the park to be deserted at the hour he'd picked, or nearly so.

All things considered, Bolan knew it was the best he could have done.

He understood that there was ample room for a double cross within the framework of his relatively simple plan. The Skulls would almost certainly turn out in force, and he was hoping for a delegation from the Savage Nomads on the side. But they might come without the girl, a trick to make him lay his weapons down perhaps. They'd soon be gravely disappointed if they went that route.

Without the girl the Executioner had no good reason for allowing any member of the gangs to live. If Corey Souders wasn't present when the meet went down, or if he had some reason to suspect that she was dead, the Executioner would leave scorched earth behind. No mercy.

The hardest part of any hostage situation was the trade, with everyone on edge, the adrenaline pumping, the potential for betrayal magnified. One slip, and you were looking at a bloodbath, everything you worked for going up in smoke.

Except this time a bloodbath was precisely what the doctor ordered. It was trickier to lift a hostage out and waste the hostage-takers at the scene, but there were ways of doing anything.

The pay phone jangled for attention, and he picked it up.

"Hello?"

"You rang?" The homicide detective's voice was weary, strained.

"You sound like you could use some sleep."

"A month might get me started. What's the word?"

"We're on for an exchange at one o'clock at Agua Vista Park."

"Who's coming?"

"Their discretion," Bolan said. "I'm hoping everybody."

"Jesus, you don't ask much, do you?"

Bolan smiled. "I'll take whatever I can get."

"This time around you might not like the choices."

"I never have."

"The girl?"

"They're bringing her supposedly. I'll have to wait and see."

"Should I expect a few more tags before the main event?"

"I won't have time," the Executioner replied. "If something's happening, it won't be me."

"Okay. What kind of lead time do you need?"

"If I can't get it done in fifteen minutes, there's no way to get it done at all."

"Sounds fair. One problem, though."

"What's that?"

"Earl Weathers in GIU. His eyes and ears inside the gangs might clue him in. I can't rule out the possibility that he might try some kind of action on his own. I'll slow him down if I get any kind of chance at all, but there might not be time."

"No sweat. I'll make allowances."

"The bluesuits won't."

"I understand."

"No way of getting Justice in on this, I guess."

"No way at all."

"I was afraid of that."

"I don't want Souders showing up and getting in the way."

"He's covered," Gibson said. "The gangs can't reach him, and he isn't going anywhere tonight."

"Okay, that's it then."

"Wait a second."

"Yes?"

The captain changed his mind. "Forget it. I'll be seeing you."

"Okay."

Bolan hung up the dead phone in his hand. He had a notion how the homicide detective felt, but there was no point in dwelling on it. The warrior long ago had come to terms with personal mortality, and he didn't confuse himself with Superman, by any means. In one sense he'd lived on borrowed time since the beginning of his one-man war against the Mafia, and having come this far was something of a miracle.

That said, he didn't yield to fatalism, sitting back and waiting for the flow of circumstance to guide his life. The warrior knew one man could make a difference, and he seized each moment as it came, refusing to adopt the role of an observer while life passed him by. First-hand experience had taught him that a man who stood his ground could sometimes change the course of history... or save a few lives at the very least.

And if some other lives were lost along the way, so be it. Bolan's enemies had known the risks when they took up a predatory life-style, feeding on their fellow man like leeches sucking out the lifeblood from a healthy body. They were vermin, in the strict sense of the term, and he'd shed no tears at their demise.

But bringing that demise about would take some luck, as well as martial skill. A string of hit-and-run attacks was one thing, bagging stationary targets, but he was about to fight a full-pitched battle with the Skulls at least on neutral ground. If Corey Souders suffered in the process, he was looking at defeat, no matter how many gang-bangers he took out.

Priorities.

It made no sense at all if you forgot the purpose of the game, and there was more to Bolan's war than making all the savages fall down.

He closed his mind to the suggestion of defeat and walked back to his car. The clock was running down, and he needed time to prep his chosen battlefield for various contingencies.

One custom-tailored bloodbath coming up.

THIS TIME she heard the footsteps coming from a greater distance, well before the jangling of the keys. Another glance around her cell reminded her unnecessarily that she was helpless.

At least her hands were free. Corey wondered if her captors would be dumb enough to stand in close and let her reach their eyes. If she could blind one, even mark his face for life, she might not feel like such a total failure when they took her down.

The door swung open to reveal the same Skull who had brought the food some hours earlier. Behind him in the hall were two other punks she didn't recognize.

"We're goin' now," the leader of the trio told her, pulling handcuffs from his pant pocket and twirling them around. "I want to see your hands behind your back."

"See this!"

She took a long step forward, leading with her left, and snapped a kick in the direction of his groin. It was a reckless move, but it was all she had, and Corey didn't feel like being manacled a second time while she had any power to resist.

The hoodlum looked surprised, but he was fast enough to dodge the kick and catch her ankle in his hands. A tug, a twist, and Corey was airborne, landing on her back with force enough to empty out her lungs. She felt as if she were drowning, dark spots swarming in the space behind her eyes as rough hands turned her over, pressing her face against the floor.

"Smart bitch! You mess with me and you're makin' one king-size mistake."

He bent her arms at painful angles, taking care to clamp the cuffs on tighter than he had to, cutting off most of the circulation to her hands. Not finished yet, he used the cuffs to lift Corey off the floor, sharp pains in her shoulder sockets causing her to cry out loud.

At least when she was screaming she could breathe.

"You want to try some more smart shit?" her captor asked. "The boys and me got time to play a little game if you want to be that way."

She shook her head, afraid to answer verbally and let him hear the tremor in her voice.

"That's better then." His smile was wicked, cold. "Why don't you move your ass before I have to kick it all the way from here out to the street?"

She did as she was told, more gang members waiting for them at the far end of the narrow corridor. One of them took a blue bandanna from his pocket, folded it to form a blindfold and secured it across her eyes. Small hope, at that, believing they wouldn't conceal their route unless there was a decent chance she might survive to tell the tale.

"Step down."

She took it slowly, letting Skulls on either side of her direct her steps and hold her upright with their hands beneath her arms. The concrete walk sloped downward toward a street or alley. There were hands all over her as Corey climbed into a waiting van, but she didn't protest.

Moments later they were moving, bodies crowded close around her, furtive hands encroaching on her space from time to time. She concentrated on the smell and sounds of weapons being readied, steel and gun oil, clacking noises as the Skulls inserted magazines and worked the cocking bolts.

She realized she was riding in the vanguard of a war machine, but there was no hope of escape.

Corey Souders was going along for the ride to the end of the line.

WHEN PLAYBOY RAYMOND finished counting heads, he knew there were twenty-seven Nomads standing armed and ready to obey his next command. Another eight or nine were on the way, but they were running late, some kind of hassle with their van, and he'd have to leave without them if they didn't show up soon.

No sweat.

With twenty-seven guns behind him—twenty eight, including T-Bone—he could damn well punch the clock on forty, maybe fifty Skulls. The odds were good that One Shot Johnson didn't even have that many soldiers left, and those that had survived the past few hours would be letting down their guard, where Playboy and the Savage Nomads were concerned.

Everybody was friendly now for the duration of the cease-fire anyway.

Like hell.

The worst mistake that Mr. Elroy Johnson ever made was thinking he could pull some kind of shit on Playboy Raymond and survive to tell the tale. It wasn't clear exactly what he had in mind, but he was clearly scamming, and the Nomads weren't about to see their territory stripped away without a fight. No way at all.

They were invited to the meet at Agua Vista Park, and they were turning out in force, but not to watch some white dude buy the farm. That would be gravy, paying back some heavy scores accumulated in the past two days, but honkies came and went. The Skulls had been a thorn in Playboy Raymond's side for the past two years, and he was ready to remove that thorn.

Tonight.

He had no plan, per se, except to watch how things went down and have his soldiers ready when he gave the word. He'd survived this long on instinct, in the joint and on the streets, with no one looking out for him except his own sweet self. Tonight he had a chance to demonstrate before his troops exactly how a general ran a war.

And it was overdue, damn right.

For the past two days he'd been losing men as if they were going out of style, and the survivors had been getting nervous. Most of them concealed it fairly well, afraid of pissing off their warlord with a show of cowardice, but you could see it in their eyes if you looked close enough. Not fear exactly, but a kind of desperation, wanting someone they could finger for the pain they'd incurred, the helpless feeling that accompanied being kicked around by someone that you couldn't even see.

They had an hour yet before the meet was scheduled, but he wanted all his people on the road in fifteen minutes. No point in dragging ass and showing up when all the fun was over. If there was a party going on, Playboy wanted his companions in the Savage Nomads to receive their share of favors, going in.

"You all know what we're on about tonight,' he told the silent ranks. "We've got some business to take care of, and before we're done, it'll all be settled with the Skulls, besides this white-bread motherfucker we've been lookin' for."

"Right on," somebody muttered from the second row.

"We've got to watch the timing on a deal like this," the warlord said. "I call the shots, and no one better make a move without I tell you first. Get eager, and you just might fuck things up for everybody down the line. Some questions?''

No one spoke or raised a hand.

"All right, then, y'all be cool. Go find your rides and keep the hardware out of sight until we get there. Move it out.''

19

It wouldn't do to mine the park or string up booby traps where innocent civilians might be killed or injured if the play went sour. Rather, Bolan spent his lead time mapping out the battlefield and plotting fire zones, picking out the cover he could count on and devising angles of retreat. With nothing left to chance Bolan knew he stood a better chance of living through the night.

The logical approach for the Executioner's enemies was China Basin Street, which formed the western boundary of the park. They might approach from north or south, but either way their vehicles would still be visible a block or two before they reached the public parking lot. An alternate approach would be across the Central Basin, using boats to reach the fishing pier, and while it seemed unlikely, Bolan couldn't absolutely rule out an amphibious assault.

He dealt with first things first, a heavy satchel charge concealed beneath the pier. There were no fishermen around at midnight, and the remote-control device he'd use to detonate the plastique was designed to screen out two-way radio transmission, signals from garage door openers and such. If it wasn't required, he could retrieve the satchel later or provide the SFPD bomb squad with directions to its hiding place.

A second charge was planted in the trunk of Bolan's car, positioned in the parking lot, its detonator keyed to an entirely different signal than the C-4 charge beneath the pier. He was prepared to sacrifice the rented wheels if necessary and escape on foot. To that end he'd hidden street clothes underneath the garbage dumpster at a supermarket three blocks south on Illinois, and likewise near a warehouse to the north along Pier 64.

For now, he wore the midnight skinsuit, his face and hands obscured with warpaint that would help him take advantage of the darkness. Underneath his arm, the sleek Beretta nestled in its shoulder sling, the mighty .44 Desert Eagle Magnum automatic riding on his hip. His military harness bore the weight of hand grenades, a ten-inch Ka-bar fighting knife and canvas pouches packed with extra magazines. Across his chest a bandolier of magazines for Bolan's M-16 was crisscrossed with a belt of 40 mm high-explosive rounds to feed the M-203 launcher mounted underneath the rifle's forward stock.

Whatever happened in the next half hour, even if he blew it, the mistake wouldn't be lack of preparation or complacency. He understood the odds against him and the risks involved, but he was pledged to go ahead, for Corey Souders's sake, and for his own.

The Skulls and Nomads had been moving toward a day of reckoning since they began their operation in the City by the Bay. That reckoning was overdue, and countless innocents had paid the price meanwhile, but it was coming now. He might not get them all, and there were other gangs around, but this would be a start.

A sudden thought intruded on the warrior's mind: suppose the Nomads chose to sit it out and let their rivals take a beating, hanging back and saving their strength to fill the vacuum when the Skulls went down in flames?

It was a possibility, but he'd have to face that problem if and when it came to pass. He'd been lucky, scoring on his first call to the Skulls, when Elroy Johnson grudingly admitted his participation in the Corey kidnap scheme. From that point on he'd ignored the Nomads, trusting in their paranoia and their new alliance with the Skulls to bring them out in force for the exchange.

If he was wrong...

A miniconvoy was approaching from the north, three cars strung out behind a van. It was the gang's idea of clever, circling around the block to make their entrance from the "wrong" direction rather than approaching straight from Hunters Point.

So much for strategy.

He watched them park, some of the faces recognized from mug shots, others strange to Bolan but displaying colors with the rest, their weapons barely hidden under baggy shirts and jackets as they assembled in the parking lot.

Corey Souders was flanked by goons, a blindfold covering the top half of her face. She was unharmed as far as he could tell with his binoculars from eighty yards away.

The Skulls were early, anxious to get started with the game. He checked his watch again and eased the safety off his M-16.

"HEADS UP FOR ANYTHING," One Shot Johnson snapped, studying the eerie nightscape of the park. Streetlights illuminated the perimeter, but shadows ruled the roost beyond a radius of fifty feet, and he was suddenly reminded of the sniper fire directed at the Nomad Compound only yesterday.

"I want the bitch up here," he called, relieved when Weed and High Test brought her front and center. He felt safer with the girl in front of him, a human shield.

"We're early yet," Weed said. "Could be the dude ain't here."

"He's here," the warlord answered, totally convinced for reasons he couldn't explain. It was a feeling, more than anything.

"Here's company," a voice said from the ranks, and everybody turned to face the new arrivals coming in.

At first he'd expected pigs, but Johnson saw it was the Nomads, five cars full. They left some distance in between their own cars and the Skull vehicles as they parked, unloading with their weapons out there in plain sight. He estimated there were twenty-five or thirty of them altogether, but he didn't bother counting heads.

"I didn't know if you were coming," Johnson said to Playboy Raymond, watching as the leader of the Savage Nomads stopped some fifteen feet away.

"We're not about to miss the biggest party of the year," Playboy replied, putting on a cocky smile.

"Looks like you brought an army."

"We're partners on this thing. I wouldn't want to let you down."

"That's good to know."

"So where's this superhonkie?" Playboy asked.

"Ain't seen him yet."

"Ain't *seen* him yet?" The Nomad leader's tone was almost mocking. "I guess we'd better start lookin' for him then."

It entered Johnson's mind to warn his longtime adversary, tell him the dude was here—that he could feel the bastard watching—but he kept his mouth shut rather than permit himself to wind up looking like a fool.

"You want to look, let's look."

"All right, my man."

"Come on, bitch." Johnson took his captive by the arm and held her close against his side. "You're comin', too."

The words were barely out before he heard a distant popping sound, and a heartbeat later one of Playboy Raymond's cars exploded into leaping flames. The shock wave took a couple of the Nomads down, and then the rest of them were running, seeking cover anywhere it could be found.

"I knew it!" Johnson snapped, the hostage cursing as he hustled her along. "I knew the fucking dude was here!"

THE HOTSHOT CALL came in at 1:07 from a late-night motorist who saw the first explosion as he passed by Agua Vista Park. It came as no surprise to Barney Gibson, burning midnight oil in Homicide, but he was pleased to note that Weathers had checked out of GIU at 10:15 p.m.

So much for competition at the moment.

Patrol cars were rolling by the time he got the word, and there was nothing he could do to slow them down. His own department was deserted at the moment, both detectives from the graveyard shift distracted by a hooker killing close to the Presidio. Recalling them would take some time, and more would be required to summon other plainclothes officers from home.

The hour worked in Bolan's favor, but he wouldn't have it all his own way now that squads were rolling.

There was still the SWAT team, constantly on call, and as the action escalated, Agua Vista Park would soon be overrun with uniforms.

The name meant "water view" in Spanish, but it sounded more like "blood view" from the first reports. The captain had no way of estimating how many gang-bangers were on the scene, or how well they were armed, but he was going to find out.

With any luck, if he was quick enough, he'd turn out to be the senior officer on-site. He couldn't turn the troops around, but he could help direct their movements once he got there, try to give the Executioner some breathing room.

He called ahead to have a driver waiting in the underground garage. The elevator seemed to take forever, and he punched the button half a dozen times before the car arrived to take him down.

Gibson's driver was a sergeant named Martinez. They'd worked together once or twice the past two years, but Gibson thought he'd been slimmer then, more hair, a tad less gray in his mustache.

Surprise.

"What's shaking, Captain?"

"Blood and thunder, Sergeant. What's your record time to Agua Vista Park?"

The sergeant grinned. "I haven't set the record yet."

"Tonight's the night."

"Yes, sir."

They made good time on Seventh, southbound to Sixteenth, and west from there until the road dead-ended into Illinois. The radio was nagging at them all the way, dispatchers calling reinforcements to the latest battle zone. A short jog south on Illinois to China Basin Street, and they could navigate by ear from that point on, with gunfire and explosions leading them directly to the park.

"Sweet Jesus!"

Cars were burning in the parking lot, and one of them blew up as Gibson's driver closed the final block. He counted six patrol cars on the scene, lights flashing competition for the leaping flames, and uniforms were fanning out in search of targets, armed with .38s and riot guns.

No SWAT so far. If he could keep the bluesuits out of Bolan's way for just a little while . . .

"Right here! Pull in!"

Martinez hit the brakes and swung the steering wheel hard right. They lost some rubber going in, but Gibson had the dashboard shotgun in his hand before the unmarked cruiser came to rest. Martinez was behind him as he struck off toward the ring of patrol cars.

A couple of the cruisers had their spotlights turned in the direction of the park, where Gibson picked out several bodies littering the grass. The sounds of automatic fire were closer now, but they didn't appear to be attracting any of the heat.

He found a sergeant of patrol crouched behind the nearest car and flashed his badge. "What's going down?"

"Some kind of rumble, best I can tell. We got a call that there were thirty, forty young black males with weapons fighting in the park. Those vehicles were shot to shit when we arrived."

"Have you got men in there?" Gibson asked, nodding toward the park where muzzle-flashes split the shadows underneath the trees.

"Not yet."

"Has anybody made the call for SWAT?"

"I did. Five minutes, give or take."

"Okay," Gibson said, picking up a glint of hope. "Here's what you do...."

IT SEEMED to Playboy Raymond as if the whole damn thing had gone to shit. One minute he was standing there and rapping with the warlord of the Skulls, next thing the cars were blown sky-high and he was running for the shadows like a little kid caught stealing penny-ante shit from the corner store.

It was hopeless, trying to command his troops when they were scattered everywhere, with automatic weapons going off on every side. It was some kind of psycho trip, with everybody firing blind except the bastard who was throwing down on them with something like a mortar, dropping high-explosive charges here and there with deadly accuracy.

Jesus! Couldn't anybody pin the bastard down? It was supposed to be one man, and they had forty-something lined up on the other side. How lucky could he be?

You didn't have to think too hard about that question, with the way things had been going for the past two days. He wasn't just a lucky bastard; he was good. Not bulletproof, okay, but he was slick enough to lead the Skulls and Nomads on a righteous runaround and having them shooting one another in the bargain while he kicked their asses time and time again.

You could admire a guy like that if you could get around the fact that he was bent on killing you.

His cover was a concrete bench, with shrubbery all around. Incoming rounds sliced through the leaves and stung his scalp with slivers of concrete. The shooter didn't have a fix on Raymond yet, but even lucky ricochets could punch your ticket if you let your guard down in the middle of a fight.

Okay.

If he couldn't command his troops effectively, what *could* he do?

The thought occurred to Playboy Raymond instantly, perhaps because it had been lurking in the shadows of his mind all night. The white dude was a problem, granted, but his impact on the local scene was momentary. Even if they missed the bastard, he'd leave one day, and after he was gone things would return to normal, Skulls and Nomads butting heads for turf and traffic.

Right.

Unless he took a chance tonight and changed the rules.

He risked a glance around the bench, slid forward on his belly toward the hedge and spent a moment checking out the action close at hand. Two Skulls were lying on the grass, say twenty feet to Playboy's left, one on his back, the other facedown in a heap. No movement there, but he could see some blood and figured both of them were dead or on the way.

So where the hell was Johnson? Hiding somewhere with the girl most likely if his yellow streak was anything like Playboy Raymond thought. He might have doubled back in the direction of the cars, except there were pigmobiles arriving now, which meant they were cut off.

No sweat.

When he was finished with his business, Playboy Raymond was prepared to split on foot if necessary. Let his people sort things out the best way that they could as long as Number One was taken care of in a pinch.

He'd arranged the lawyers, front their bail and have them sailing soon enough.

But first he had some business to take care of in the park.

He caught a glimpse of movement, forty feet away and to his front. The girl! She wriggled out of cover, rising to a crouch and braced to run before an arm snaked out and hauled her back.

That made it Elroy.

Creeping forward, Playboy Raymond had a Llama automatic in his fist. Forget about the grass stains on his jacket and khakis; he could buy himself a thousand outfits with the income from their first month's traffic once the Skulls were busted out.

While he was at it he could do the girl. No witnesses, no case.

He kept his eyes fixed on a low break in the shrubs where Corey Souders had appeared and vanished moments earlier. They could be moving granted, but it wouldn't matter much. How far could Elroy travel in the bushes with a squirming bitch to slow him down?

Just far enough to make it sporting, maybe.

Playboy Raymond felt an urge to laugh, but he restrained himself. Around him men were dying for their cliques, and there was nothing humorous in that... especially when he could still be one of them.

He reached the clearing in the bushes, wriggled through and was about to push up on his hands and knees when someone pressed the muzzle of a gun behind his ear.

"What you be lookin' for?"

There was no mistaking Johnson's voice.

"Same thing as you," the warlord of the Nomads said. "Some cover, man."

"Too bad you didn't make it, cuz."

Playboy thought his life should flash before his eyes, but there was only panic, forcing him to roll away and thrust the pistol out in front of him, his finger tightening around the trigger.

Too damn late.

The first round struck him in the throat, and he was drowning, trying desperately to draw a final breath. He felt the Llama tumble from his spastic fingers, gone, and there was nothing more he could do to save himself.

THE EXECUTIONER lost track of all the Skulls and Nomads he'd killed since it had begun. The M-16 was on its fourth replacement magazine, and he'd used up half the 40 mm ammunition in his bandolier, destroying vehicles, demolishing a rest room where a number of his adversaries had tried to hide, uprooting clumps of shrubbery where they had gone to ground.

They almost seemed intent on getting killed, as if a head-on charge would do the job on nerve alone. He changed positions frequently to keep them guessing, but they homed in on his muzzle-flashes, coming after him by threes and fours while Bolan chewed them up and spit them out again.

The cops were hanging back so far, but Bolan knew it wouldn't last. As soon as someone in authority arrived, or they were issued riot gear, the bluesuits would be coming in. From that point on there would be no way for him to control the action, nothing he could do to keep police from getting killed.

He needed a diversion, something that would draw a number of the opposition off or give them cause to hesitate. He reached down for the detonator on his belt and flicked up the switch to arm the proper charge.

On three.

When the numbers counted down, he keyed the C-4 charge and heard the fishing pier disintegrate, jagged scraps of lumber spinning skyward in a ball of flame. Almost at once a dozen thugs or more were up and running toward the scene of the explosion, drawn like insects to a night light, several of them firing on the run. Offshore he saw police boats closing in to slam the back door on their prey.

And hanging back, way to Bolan's left, the warlord of the Skulls stood watching, holding Corey Souders by one arm.

The warrior circled wide to come up on the gangster's blind side, closing rapidly with measured strides. He flicked the M-16's selective fire switch onto semiautomatic as he made the move and had the weapon braced against his shoulder, sighting, when he spoke. "Looks like we're all alone."

The young man swung around to face him, dragging Corey Souders in between them, with his pistol pressed against her spine. She had a slightly dazed look on her face, and it was impossible to say if she was injured, drugged or merely dazed.

"You be the man?"

"It looks that way."

"That's pretty slick, you sucker all those guys away like that."

"I thought we ought to have some time alone."

"This was supposed to be a trade."

"I changed my mind."

"Bad business, welchin' out that way."

"I guess you meant to play it straight?"

The grin on Johnson's face looked natural, like it belonged there. Under different circumstances he could easily have passed for something else.

A human being, right.

"Doesn't matter what I had in mind. We're down to cases now."

"It looks that way."

"You want this bitch, or what?"

"That isn't any way to talk about a lady," Bolan told the warlord of the Skulls.

And shot him dead-on.

A single 5.5 mm tumbler closed the gap between them, clipped a lock of Corey Souders's hair and punched a hole where Elroy Johnson's nose had been a hearbeat earlier. The hydrostatic shock of impact pulped his brain and hurled him backward, cutting off the signal that would send a bullet into Corey's back.

When Bolan reached her, she was trembling, winding up a scream that would have given competition to the sirens drawing closer all around. He put an arm around her shoulders, pulled her close and cautioned her to keep it down.

"My father?"

"Waiting for you back at home."

"Can we...?"

"Not we," he said. "The uniforms will get you there. I need to take a walk."

"You're not...I mean...you saved my life."

"We'll talk about it someday when we have the time."

She turned away, still looking dazed.

"Make sure you let them see your hands."

She raised both arms above her head and kept on walking. Bolan watched her for another moment before he turned and ran to find the dark.

EPILOGUE

Two warriors stood above the Golden Gate at dawn. The sea was dark and cold, as yet untouched by morning light. The older of the two men wore a trench coat and a rumpled business suit; his companion looked athletic in a sport coat over shirt and slacks. The wind played with their hair and tried to whip their words away.

"The girl?"

"Hospital checked her out and sent her home. I figure she could help us make a case if we had anybody left to prosecute."

"That clean?"

"Not quite. We picked up seventeen, and some of those are wounded. Mainly grunts. We'll let her take a look when things calm down, but it's a long shot, making any of the small-fry."

"You should have enough to tie them up a fair while, as it is," Bolan said.

"Hey, no sweat. Between the weapons charges and resisting, some attempted murders here and there, I'm thinking all of them should do some time."

"So it's a fair day's work."

"Two days," Barney Gibson told him. "Two *long* days. I don't need any more like this."

"I'll make a note."

"I wish you would. What's next?"

"Another front."

"It must get old."

"Oh, yeah?"

The homicide detective thought about it, smiling to himself.

"Or maybe not."

"About Souders..."

"If you're thinking gang retaliation, let it go. Between the Skulls and Nomads on the street, they couldn't field a decent softball team. The ones we missed don't know their ass from Tuesday, much less what's been going on with Souders."

"Fair enough."

"One thing," the captain said. "You do light up the town."

"Too much, I guess."

"It helps out every now and then. Keeps everybody on their toes."

"Including you?"

"Especially me." A silent moment passed, then Gibson said, "I'm bailing out, you know."

"Good luck."

"I wonder if I'll miss it sometimes. Hell, no reason why I should."

"You've done your bit."

"And you?"

"I don't have much of a retirement plan."

"You ought to check that out."

"I'll see what I can do."

"I'm sure."

"If you run into Souders..."

"Yeah?"

"Forget it."

"Right."

"Maybe I'll see you."

"Maybe so."

The warriors turned their backs on darkness, separating as they moved back toward the light of day.

These heroes can't be beat!

Celebrate the American hero with this collection of never-before-published installments of America's finest action teams—ABLE TEAM, PHOENIX FORCE and VIETNAM: GROUND ZERO—only in Gold Eagle's

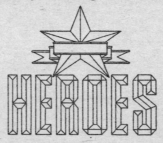

Available for the first time in print, eight new hard-hitting and complete episodes of America's favorite heroes are contained in three action-packed volumes:

In **HEROES: Book I**   July $5.99   592 pages

ABLE TEAM: Razorback by Dick Stivers
PHOENIX FORCE: Survival Run by Gar Wilson
VIETNAM: GROUND ZERO: Zebra Cube by Robert Baxter

In **HEROES: Book II**   August $5.99   592 pages

PHOENIX FORCE: Hell Quest by Gar Wilson
ABLE TEAM: Death Lash by Dick Stivers
PHOENIX FORCE: Dirty Mission by Gar Wilson

In **HEROES: Book III**   September $4.99   448 pages

ABLE TEAM: Secret Justice by Dick Stivers
PHOENIX FORCE: Terror in Warsaw by Gar Wilson

Celebrate the finest hour of the American hero with your copy of the Gold Eagle HEROES collection.

Available in retail stores in the coming months.   HEROES

**A twenty-first century commando meets his
match on a high-tech battlefield.**

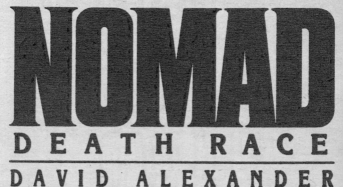

NOMAD
DEATH RACE
DAVID ALEXANDER

He's called Nomad—a new breed of commando battling
the grim forces of techno-terrorism that threaten the
newfound peace of the twenty-first century.

In DEATH RACE, the second title in the NOMAD series,
the KGB is conspiring to bring America to her knees. A
supersoldier clone—Nomad's double—has been
programmed with a devastating termination directive.
Nomad becomes a hunted man in a cross-country death
race that leads to the prime target—the White House.

For the eternal soldier, Dan Samson, the battle has shifted to the Mexican-American war in Book 2 of the time-travel miniseries . . .

TIMERAIDER

John Barnes

Dan Samson, a hero for all time, is thrown back to the past to fight on the battlefields of history.

In Book 2: BATTLECRY, Dan Samson faces off against deadly enemies on both sides of the conflict—ready to forfeit his life to ensure the course of destiny.

Available in August at your favorite retail outlet.